The Burning of the *General Slocum*

The wreck of the General Slocum, *where she sank after the fire. Her starboard paddle wheel remained above water, marking her grave.*

THE BURNING OF THE

General Slocum

BY

CLAUDE RUST

E L S E V I E R / N E L S O N   B O O K S
New York

974.7
Rust

LIBRARY OF CONGRESS CATALOGING IN PUBLICATION DATA

Rust, Claude.
The burning of the General Slocum.

Bibliography: p.
Includes index.
Summary: Describes the 1904 fire aboard the excursion
steamship *General Slocum* in New York City's East River
in which more than 1000 passengers died of burns and
drowning.
1. General Slocum (Steamboat) 2. New York (N.Y.)—
Fire, 1904. [1. General Slocum (Steamboat) 2. New
York (N.Y.)—Fire, 1904] I. Title.
F128.5R92   974.1'1   81–3202
ISBN 0-525-66715-6   AACR2

Published in the United States by Elsevier-Dutton Publishing Co., Inc.,
2 Park Avenue, New York, N.Y. 10016. Published simultaneously in
Canada by Clarke, Irwin & Company
Limited, Toronto and Vancouver
Designer: Trish Parcell

Printed in the U.S.A.   First edition
10 9 8 7 6 5 4 3 2 1

To my Grandmother, Charlotte May, and all the others who died on the *General Slocum* that day.

CONTENTS

1904	1
Little Germany	15
Siebzehnte Wasserfahrt	20
The Lost Moments	35
Pandemonium	44
The Flotilla	73
Kahnweiler's Never Sink Life Preservers	83
The Aftermath	94
The Inquest	109
The Fate of the Captain and His Ship	127
The Report	130
APPENDIX	
General Slocum Statistics	139
Roster of the Crew	140
BIBLIOGRAPHY	141
INDEX	145

Illustrations appear on pages 11 – 14, 38 – 39,
63 – 72, and 105 – 108

Yes, Sir. Terrible affair that *General Slocum* explosion. Terrible, terrible! A thousand casualties. And heart rending scenes. Men trampling down women and children. Most brutal thing. What do they say was the cause? Spontaneous combustion: most scandalous revelation. Not a single lifeboat would float and the firehose all burst. What I can't understand is how the inspectors ever allowed a boat like that . . . Now you are talking straight, Mr. Crimmins. You know why? Palmoil. Is that a fact? Without a doubt . . .

Graft, my dear sir. Well, of course, where there's money going there's always someone to pick it up.

JAMES JOYCE, Ulysses

The Burning of the *General Slocum*

1904

IN THE UNITED STATES, it was a button-busting year. The people — still flushed with the victories of their far-flung war with Spain — reveled in the leadership of Teddy Roosevelt. The pistol-packing President stood for no nonsense. While he fought corruption at home with the Big Stick of antitrust laws, he was protesting loudly the detention of two Americans abroad: Jack London by the Japanese and Ion Perdicaris by a Moroccan brigand named Ahmad-ibn-Muhammad Raisuli. Secretary of State John Hay sent a ringing telegram to the American consul in Morocco: "We want Perdicaris alive or Raisuli dead." The detention of London turned out to be a mistake, and two days after Hay's cable, Perdicaris was released.

It was a time for plain unadulterated patriotism. Hats off! Bully! And all that.

It was a time for Victor Herbert, Fritzi Scheff, the Floradora

1

girls. For the rich it was Madison Square Garden, the horse show in the fall, the opera in the winter. For rich and poor alike, there was Ethel Barrymore in *Sunday* at the Hudson Theatre and Maude Adams in *The Pretty Sister of José* at the Empire. It was to be the year when *Rebecca of Sunnybrook Farm* and *Beverly of Graustark* would be shaken from their literary perches by the brutal Wolf Larsen, stalking across the pages of Jack London's *Sea Wolf*.

Coupons were given out to promote the sale of cigarettes, and women were arrested for smoking in public. Installment buying was encouraged, especially for the purchase of diamonds. The country was expanding, and New York with it. The move was uptown. The Times building was going up, and a few blocks north, the fabulous Hotel Astor. At Thirty-third and Seventh, a magnificent colonnaded structure of granite and marble rose: the terminal for the far-spreading Pennsylvania Railroad.

These were the good old days. There was plenty of work. You made only ten or twenty a week, but it went a long way. It was the day of the two-cent stamp, the penny postcard, the five-cent beer, and ten-cent shot. For the more discriminating there were cocktails at fifteen cents — two for a quarter. Potatoes were one cent a pound, pork, twelve cents a pound. Men's suits were twelve dollars, shoes two, add a dollar for a straw skimmer, and you were off on an all-day excursion aboard the *General Slocum*.

It was the heyday of the excursion. You packed a lunch basket, donned your straw skimmer, took the children by the hand — or perhaps your best girl — and were off to a nearby pier. A sleek white side-wheeler, crowded with other holiday merrymakers, picked you up, and you were whisked off for a day's outing — a cool walk on the breezy promenade, perhaps a waltz on the afterdeck to the tune of a band, or just a restful lounge in a wicker chair while the panorama of the shore moved past. Eventually you would arrive at a picnic grounds along the Hudson River or the green Long Island shore, some of them laid out and maintained by the steamboat companies for the very purpose of luring you out of the hot city, and there you could stroll or play ball or simply eat your picnic lunch in peace until it was time to board the steamer for the return trip.

In 1904 at least a dozen excursion vessels plied the waters of New York Harbor and its adjacent rivers, straits, and inlets. In the days before vehicular bridges and parkways and automobiles made it possible for families to go on private outings, the excursion boat was the best possible way to escape the summer heat and the everyday grind. The poor, the middle classes, the bulk of the city's population who owned no summer homes, no yachts, no private beaches — for them the excursion boat was a kind of personification of summer.

But 1904 was to give people a whole new idea of excursion boats. . . .

On May 5 of that boisterous year, two men boarded an excursion steamer at a Brooklyn pier to carry out the vessel's annual inspection. In preparation for the upcoming season, the *General Slocum* had received a new coat of gleaming white, covering much of its originally varnished woodwork. Her smokestacks, painted yellow, had by now become baked to a patina of warm buff by the heat from below. The machinery had been checked, the steering gear tested, and the *Slocum* appeared like a bright new boat ready for her best season yet.

Or so her owners hoped. For the *Slocum* had had a somewhat checkered career during her thirteen years of carrying excursionists to Rockaway Beach. Misfortune had started on her very first summer.

That was in 1891, when she was fresh off the Devine-Burtis ways in Red Hook, Brooklyn. She had been built as the sister ship of the Knickerbocker Steamboat Company's older excursion vessel *Grand Republic*. She was somewhat shorter than the

3

older ship — 264 feet from the fluttering flag at her prow to the fluttering flag at her stern — but stronger, trimmer, and swifter. The hull had been strengthened by a special series of fore-and-aft running braces, and she was fitted with a new type of steam steering gear that enabled one helmsman to manage the largest vessel. Amidships, she carried twin paddle wheels fitted with machinery at the W. A. Fletcher yards in Hoboken.

The Knickerbocker Company had ordered that their vessel was to be elegant as well as powerful, so the *Slocum's* hull had been painted a shining white, the masts and stacks yellow, and all the rest was varnished wood — rails, cabins, paddle boxes — everything. The grand saloons on her two lower decks — lower or main, middle or promenade — were finished in polished mahogany and sycamore, with plate-glass mirrors between the windows, fancy wood carvings, and rich carpets throughout. The promenade saloon, 100 feet long, was furnished with summery wickerwork and finished in red velvet.

After debating a number of different names — Columbus, Knickerbocker, Rockaway, Brooklyn — the company decided to name the vessel after a local hero and politician: Major General Henry Warner Slocum (1827–1894), who had commanded the right wing of the Union Army at Gettysburg, followed Sherman to the sea, and served three terms in Congress, representing Brooklyn. So, as the *General Slocum* she was launched.

For the first two months, the *Slocum* had smooth sailing. Of the three trips a day offered by the company on Saturdays and Sundays, the *Slocum* usually made two, leaving the New York pier at 8:40 A.M. and returning immediately from Rockaway at 11:30, to make ready for her second run at 1:30, which returned to New York at 6:30 P.M. The middle run, which left New York at 10 A.M. and returned at 4 P.M., was handled by the Slocum's sister ship, *Grand Republic*. From time to time these assignments were reversed, but usually the *Slocum's* popularity prevailed and she was put back on two runs a day. The fare was

4

fifty cents for a round trip, which took about two and a half hours. Most excursionists, to enjoy the day fully and get the most for their half dollar, would take the *Slocum* out on her first morning run and return on her last evening trip to New York; it was nice to go out early, spend the day on the Rockaway beaches, and steam home in late afternoon.

But then, on August 14, 1891, the *Slocum* ran aground on a bar near Rockaway, and three days later she backed into a Sandy Hook steamer. No one was hurt during these two foul-ups, but they were the first of a series of mishaps that were to plague her.

For the seasons of 1892 and 1893, the *Slocum*'s career was untroubled. Indeed, she was a popular, even fashionable vessel. The excursion season always started for her with a Decoration Day trip to Bridgeport, Connecticut, an annual event so popular that passengers boasted of having been able to make it.

The second highlight of the harbor's summer was the International Yacht Races off Sandy Hook, a great occasion for sailing enthusiasts and the general public alike. The *General Slocum*, being one of the swifter ships in the harbor, was very much in demand among spectators, and large sums were bid for chartering her. On yacht-race day the *Slocum* became a seagoing grandstand, every available spot on the favored side filled with cheering humanity and the top deck crammed to the smokestacks. Sportsmen improvised "box seats" in the lifeboats and rafts, sat atop the captain's cabin and the pilothouse, balanced on the paddle box, and perched like blackbirds on the hogback frame. On these occasions, the side-wheeler showed a decided list to the crowded side, where one overworked wheel — biting deep into the brine — forced feathers of spume from the paddle-box breather holes.

And in between such special occasions she carried ordinary excursion crowds on her regularly advertised routes between Manhattan and Rockaway.

5

Then came the disastrous season of 1894. In the early weeks, she ran aground twice, and on July 29 rammed into a sandbar so hard that several of her supporting stanchions were broken and 250 electric lights went out, sending passengers into a panic. (It was said that there were almost 4,700 persons aboard on this trip, double the limit allowed by law.) Two weeks later she went aground again in heavy weather, forcing the crew to summon a fishing boat to take off some passengers and stranding those who remained for over twenty-four hours.

When the *Slocum* was safely back in her berth, her master, Captain William Van Schaick, stoutly defended her performance. "She is not taking a drop of water," he announced, "and will go on her regular run. I think the *General Slocum* is the greatest wooden ship afloat."

Some people were beginning to have their doubts — especially when the excursion boat had still another accident that same season. As she was backing out into the East River on September 1, a tugboat smashed into her stern, cutting her rudder post and leaving her to drift helplessly until two other vessels came to her rescue.

The following three seasons were relatively uneventful, marred only by an occasional fine for overcrowding. Then, on July 9, 1898, while Americans were celebrating their recent victory over the inept Spanish fleet outside Santiago de Cuba, disaster struck the *Slocum* again. With two hundred passengers aboard, she was rounding the Battery against an ebbing tide. Suddenly the lighter *Amelia* appeared off the *Slocum's* port bow, and after a confused mix-up of signals, the big excursion boat rammed the *Amelia* amidships.

Barrels of sugar rumbled off the lighter's broad deck, passengers on the *Slocum* panicked, and the vessels drifted downstream, locked in an unmanageable mass. Off Pier 6, the *Slocum* finally won clear and was able to complete her run with only a small hole in her bow. But the *Amelia* had to beach herself on Governor's Island, and once more the excursion boat had earned herself a bad name.

Thereafter, ill luck began to crowd in on her: trouble with the walking beam, buckets breaking on both wheels, endless mechanical breakdowns. Though she was only seven years old, her popularity was fading along with the red velvet in the promenade saloon. There were no more generous bids for her services at the yacht races. She was slowly edged out by more seaworthy and faster screw steamers. Little by little she became the working man's transport, and her history had become so synonymous with misfortune that the public automatically thought of her when there was a harbor accident.

On July 14, 1901, the steamer *Julia*, operating between Canarsie and Rockaway, ran aground with several hundred passengers aboard. Somehow or other, word got out that, while the *Julia* was stranded, the *General Slocum* had grazed her. Another popular version was that the two vessels had collided, and one of them was sinking. In spite of this, the *Slocum's* crew maintained that, not only had they not collided with the *Julia*, they had not even sighted her.

A month later the vessel was in real trouble. Among her excursionists that day was a party of ironworkers from Paterson, New Jersey, on a day's outing. Some of them were drunk and surly, and by the time the vessel reached the Narrows, they exploded into open fighting. The brawl began on the lower deck but was soon carried to the upper deck, where the women and children had taken refuge. Fists flew, then glasses, bottles, camp stools, and everything else not tied down. Women screamed, children panicked. Finally Van Schaick turned out the crew.

That marked a turn in the battle. The drunken ironworkers were slowly driven back into a cabin and subdued. Seven were tied up and dragged down to the hold, and the *Slocum* entered Jamaica Bay with her whistles calling for help.

7

A police launch came alongside and removed the seven prisoners, then surged ahead to summon reserves from the Rockaway station house to meet the vessel as it docked. A single gangplank was thrown out, and passengers straggled shakily off. Four more culprits were spotted among them and arrested, the remainder treated for injuries and allowed to continue their by-now-ruined holiday. On the return trip, a detail of police from the West Twentieth Street station in Manhattan escorted the unlucky craft to Jersey City, where the rest of the Paterson party was landed.

The next year, 1902, there were more accidents. On June 15, steaming into Jamaica Bay in thick gray fog, the *Slocum* suddenly found herself in the path of an oncoming yacht. She sheered off to avoid a collision and ran up on a shifting sandbar two hundred feet. With the tide ebbing, she was stuck there for the night, and the company — by now apprehensive about its reputation — sent the stranded passengers home by rail. Two weeks later the *Slocum* collided with another excursion boat while the two were trying to dock at the same pier.

Now, two seasons later, the veteran ship had been prepared for a fresh start. And the first item on her agenda was passing inspection by federal agents, charged with certifying her as fit to carry 2,500 passengers on the "bays and harbors of New York and the tributaries thereto."

Responsible for this inspection was the U.S. Steamboat Inspection Service, a bureau of the Department of Commerce, which was headed by nine regional supervising inspectors appointed by the President. These supervising inspectors appointed district inspectors to oversee operations within a specific port, and the district inspectors in turn named local men, who were charged with inspecting hulls, boilers, and safety equipment of steam-operated vessels. The locals were paid on a piecework basis — so much for each inspection, regardless of how thorough.

Politics had crept into the service, however — 1904 was also the heyday of graft, corruption, and muckraking — and local and district inspectors were appointed more often because they were candidates of some powerful precinct captain than because they knew much about hulls, boilers, and safety equipment. Inevitably the service had deteriorated, until by 1904 the supervising inspectors were not supervising, the district inspectors were not overseeing, and the local inspectors were doing as little inspecting as possible.

The two agents aboard the *Slocum* would divide up the present inspection between them. John Fleming, assistant inspector of boilers, would see to mechanical equipment. The soundness of the safety equipment and the vessel's seaworthiness were the responsiblity of Henry Lundberg, assistant inspector of hulls, a sullen, round-faced man of thirty-four.

After passing "a splendid civil service examination," as one of his superiors put it, Lundberg had made tours of inspection with five different men to learn the ropes. That was his training. After a few weeks of observing on the job, he had been declared competent to pass judgment on the safety of a steamboat. Once he had sweated out a probationary period, Lundberg was assured of a civil-service appointment and its subsequent ironclad contract for a virtually unlosable job.

After taking leave of Fleming, Lundberg picked up Chief Engineer Ben Conklin, a veteran of thirteen years aboard the *Slocum*, and First Mate Ed Flanagan. Swaggering about the vessel with a stick in hand, Lundberg poked at the life belts overhead. They were stored behind slats nailed to the overhead carlings along the lower deck. Each belt was required by law to contain six pounds of solid cork. On Lundberg's order Ed Flanagan took down some belts for closer scrutiny. Lundberg marked them all "up to date and of good quality" on Steamboat

9

Inspection Service Form 922. On his turn around the main deck, Lundberg opened and shut the standpipe valves to the fire lines, a test he deemed sufficient whether water came through or not. Chief Engineer Conklin could have filled these pipes with water by turning one wheel at the donkey engine, but Lundberg did not ask him to.

The fire hoses — coiled neatly, but almost out of reach above the standpipes — were assumed to be serviceable. On Form 923, spaces were allotted for "length of hose," "pressure per square inch," and other time-consuming tests, but Lundberg merely scribbled in what so many other inspectors had scribbled: "in good condition." On the promenade deck a few more life belts were poked at, then Lundberg made his way to the top deck. That was where the *Slocum* carried her six lifeboats — four of them standing under davits swung inboard, all tied down and glued to their chocks with thick white paint. On Form 923 he noted the six as "swung under davits" — that is, suspended in air and ready for emergency launching. After a cursory examination of the hull, the inspection was over.

As Lundberg and Fleming left the *General Slocum*, powdered cork peppered the newly varnished decks — powdered cork from the thousands of life belts dated "1891."

The General Slocum *in better days, seen against the Manhattan skyline around the turn of the century.*

Close-up of the General Slocum, *one of the most popular excursion boats plying New York Harbor during the 1890's.*

Anchored on the Hudson during one of her excursion trips.

The General Slocum
rounding the Battery.

*St. Mark's Evangelical
Lutheran Church.*

Pages of the excursion program welcoming guests to St. Mark's seventeenth annual boat trip.

The Reverend George F. Haas. His wife and daughter perished in the fire.

LITTLE GERMANY

FIVE WEEKS AFTER the inspection that qualified the *General Slocum* as an excursion boat in public service, she was chartered for a day's outing by St. Mark's Evangelical Lutheran Church on Sixth Street. St. Mark's seventeenth annual excursion to Locust Grove on Long Island Sound, to be held on June 15, 1904, was the talk of that bit of Manhattan known as Little Germany.

This neighborhood, running along the East River from Houston to Fourteenth Streets, then held a predominantly German population, many of them recent immigrants. Steerage rates for the London–New York run had recently been reduced to an unbelievable ten dollars, and this cheap fare had lured as many as forty thousand people to this country only the year before.

Nevertheless, Little Germany was no slum. Its population

had brought skills and ambition from the Old World, and the area bristled with small shops and one-man businesses. Peter Schneider, manufacturer and dealer in cider, had his *Stube,* or bar, just across the street from St. Mark's Church itself. Georg Junge operated an ice-cream saloon around the corner on First Avenue, where you could buy an ice-cream soda for five cents. For the hungry, there was Eugen Ansel's delicatessen on Fourth Street or Gus Neugebauer's butcher shop up the block. For the smoker there was Henry Jordan's cigar store on Third Avenue. For other needs you visited or called in Hannemann the plumber, Hedenkamp the carpenter, Schnitzerling the painter, or Hermann the florist. People rose, worked hard all day, and came home to their families at night.

A few of the buildings in the neighborhood were old, predating the Civil War — tired, plain old structures with unadorned facades and low-ceilinged rooms. But the keynote of the area was a more recent and exuberant style of architecture. The "better class" of people — doctors, dentists, brewmasters — lived in elegant sandstone houses along St. Mark's Place, which displayed high stoops and fanlights over heavily paneled doors. Working men and their families occupied most of the tall tenements on other streets, many with shops and businesses occupying the ground floor.

Doorways here were a jumble of columns, pilasters, and capitals, and upper stories were capped with cornices of every size and shape. Architects of this enclave drew from their grab bags every imaginable style — Greek, Tuscan, Moorish — to create busy amalgams of brick and stone. Above the keystones of windows scowled crudely carved pagan gods; from the corbels beneath the sills, gargoyles snarled. Even the spandrels were not spared. Above the arches over each door and window, sunbursts, leaf sprays, and filigree work appeared, and in the spaces between windows, there were faces, festoons, and arabesques, covering every inch in bas-relief — all this framed

16

in dentil, egg-dart, and a dozen other moldings, garnished lavishly with acanthus leaves. And when such a hodgepodge was completed, its builder liked to carve its date proudly in a prominent spot: 1875 . . . 1880 . . . 1885. . . .

On June 14, a Tuesday, in buildings like these all over Little Germany, the bustle of preparation was in evidence, preparation for the St. Mark's *Siebzehnte Wasserfahrt.* The bathtub in the kitchen was uncovered for that torture that preceded any midweek event, the weekday bath. When the tub had been filled, the children took turns, according to age, sex, and cleanliness — the cleanest going first, and the parade continuing till the water reached a predetermined color, when it was changed for the next batch. The trip to the water closet in the hall followed the bath. Here the imps whispered excitedly over the joys of tomorrow with the children of the other three families with whom they shared this modern convenience. Then, as they were hustled off to bed one by one, the tenements quieted down. By nightfall there were only the whisperings of the elders in the stairwells, and the talk of those sitting on the stoops outside.

At the corner of Mangin Street near the East River, the men of the neighborhood were lifting a stein or two at Ferdinand Frese's Saloon. Frese sold "Consumers Park Beer, Ales, and Liquors," and had good cigars available for his customers, who liked to drop in for a glass and a smoke after their twelve-hour working day. Most of the men at Frese's could not take time off to make tomorrow's excursion, but their families could. The thought of a carefree day for *die Frauen und Kinder* raised the level of joviality.

The singing, laughter, and *Prosits* carried up to the room above, where the owner's daughter Anna sat by the window. Though only fourteen, Anna was an accomplished pianist. After nine years of study at Steinway Hall on Fourteenth

17

Street, she had given her first concert there and afterward had been feted at Luchow's Restaurant across the street, a favorite place of the German folk thereabout. Anna looked across the Houston Street Ferry House Plaza to the long, covered recreation pier at Third Street, where the *General Slocum* would dock the next day. Beyond, in her imagination, she could see Locust Grove, a picnic area near Northport in Suffolk County, Long Island — the picnic tables heavily laden with *yiele gute Dinge zu essen,* men in endless rounds of pinochle, and her friends playing games. And the steamy streets of Little Germany forty miles away. It would be a wonderful day.

Mary Abendschein, chairwoman of the picnic committee, had other thoughts. At her home on East Eighteenth Street she did not muse on the joys of picnicking but worried about the weather, the children, the food, the music, and everything else that came to mind. Thirty-four and single, Mary had turned to church work to fill her lonely hours. She had trudged from Balser's Pharmacy on Avenue B and Ninth to Adickes Ice Cream Parlor on Avenue A, selling space in the excursion program. Succumbing to her blandishments, merchants bought a third, a sixth, or a twelfth of a page for an ad or even an anonymous *"Von einem Freund"* (From a Friend). One of the advertisers, "William Sierichs, Bottlers of Mineral Water, Genuine Ginger Ale, etc.," had not only taken an ad but had generously contributed a supply of soda pop for the occasion. Now that all the arrangements had been made, the program filled, the tickets sold, and a hundred other details attended to, Mary turned her anxious mind to matters that could not be arranged or "attended to." What was the worst thing that could happen? Oh, yes, of course, it might *rain.*

Across Manhattan, as the *General Slocum* lay at its berth on the North River and Fiftieth Street, a heavy dray clattered off cobblestoned Twelfth Avenue and rumbled across the waterfront planking to the recreation pier. The men on the wagon were from St. Mark's parish, here to deliver three barrels of drinking glasses for the festivities the next day. As they carried their fragile burdens up the gangplank, Deckhand Dan O'Neill hailed them forward to the door of the main deck saloon. There he slid back the door and helped them inside. At the bar the glasses were unpacked, and the men said good night.

O'Neill was now left with the three barrels of salt hay in which the glasses had been packed. Where should he put them? The forward cabin was where everybody threw his junk. Yes, that would do.

By rights, they should have been set ashore, since there was a regulation against carrying loose hay on steamboats. But that was a lot of trouble, and nobody made much fuss about technicalities aboard the *Slocum* — the captain was above mere details like that, the first mate didn't care, and the inspectors never brought up minor points. What about the forward cabin?

O'Neill rolled the barrels forward, slid back the door leading down to the forward cabin, and stepped inside. With each barrel he backed carefully down the steep steps and placed it just inside the door in the hold; then, before leaving, he probed deep into the hay for any glasses that might have been forgotten. As he left, the hay clinging to his sleeves scattered over the cabin floor.

SIEBZEHNTE
WASSERFAHRT

THE NEXT DAY, June 15, 1904, the sun rose at 4:20 A.M. The tide was out. The bay was calm, the East River still, and even Hell Gate was taking its allotted few minutes of quiet. The Hudson was flowing down to the sea, as a river should, carrying the sweet waters of its kills, creeks, and rivers past the towers of Manhattan. In its cold green waters, the great white side-wheeler, bathed in the morning mist, lay motionless at her mooring. Beads of dew glistened along her halyards, stays, and fall ropes dangling from the davits. The cool fresh morning air, scented with salt, filled the cabins and promenades, cleansing the decks, walls, ceilings.

Two hours after sunrise, the porter, Walter Payne, plodded through the main saloon toward the forward cabin to start his day's chores. First he had to fill the ship's oil lanterns. As he descended the steep stairway into the hold, a faint glow from the storeroom brightened into a blinding glare. The oiler from the engine room was there, working on the steam steering gear. He glanced up at the face of the black man, shining in the light of the open torch nearby, then went back to work. Payne inspected the crew's wash, hanging to dry over the hot steering mechanism, then turned away from the painful glare to find his way to the worktable against the starboard wall. As his eyes adjusted to the darkness of the rest of the cabin, the jumble around him emerged from the shadows. The room was a mass of old life belts, camp chairs, hawsers, hose, spare paddle buckets, and bags of charcoal. Besides these, Payne had to squeeze past the barrels of hay left by Deckhand O'Neill the night before.

Once at the table he cleared away the paint pots and brushes to make room for the ship's lanterns. After lighting one for himself, he blew out the match and proceeded to fill the lanterns from the oil drums along the wall. Occasionally, as he misjudged their capacity, oil trickled to the hay-strewn floor. In half an hour Payne finished his first task of the day. Cleaning up as best he could, he left the oiler at work in the warm, steamy room and climbed the eight steps up into the cool morning air in the main-deck saloon. After picking up his shoeshine box from one of the closets near the paddle-box housing, he made his way aft. It was 7 A.M.

Those of the crew who had stayed aboard were already at work. The others, the deckhands picked from waterfront streets and taverns by First Mate Flanagan, plus stewards and waiters hired haphazardly by the Knickerbocker Steamboat Company, were drifting up the gangplank for another day's pay.

Except for the captain, pilots, and engineers, most of the crew were seasonal workers taken on for the summer. Even

First Mate Ed Flanagan, a former ironworker, could boast only two seasons aboard, and Deckhand John Coakley had been hired only eighteen days before. It was a landlubber crew, unused to the steamboat trade. This year, the usual complement had been raised from 23 to 35 by the hiring of 12 extras in the steward's department, all to give the public what it demanded: service. There were now six waiters, one steward, one porter, two bartenders, a pantry man, plus a coffee man and a chowder man to serve their steaming specialties in shiny white crockery. In addition, two black stewardesses tended to the needs of female passengers.

In leisurely fashion, the crew began to prepare the *Slocum* for her day's work, arranging deck chairs and saloon tables, running up the decorative bunting that gave the vessel its festive air, hauling out equipment. The decks were washed with water from a dockside hydrant. Using the hydrant saved a trip to the donkey engine and the tiresome effort of turning on the fire-line valve, breaking out the rubber hose, and adjusting its special coupling to the fire-line standpipe. Besides, fresh water was not as hard on the deck finish as salt.

By now the oiler had finished his work on the steering gear in the forward cabin, and in the boiler room just behind a thin bulkhead, the two firemen on duty were biting into a mountain of coal to feed the two hungry furnaces. Farther aft, Chief Engineer Ben Conklin watched as steam pressure rose on the engine room gauge, waiting for the twenty-eight pounds needed to roll the big engine. Conklin, who was in his forties, had been with the ship from her launching. Of his twenty years aboard steamers, he had spent thirteen belowdecks on *Slocum*.

As the heat came up, Conklin wiped the sweat from his poached-egg eyes and double chin and nodded to his assistant, Everett Brandow, who had been with him for six seasons now. Both were from Catskill, a village on the upper Hudson; both had talked long hours about the wonders and power of steam and spent many a Busman's Holiday visiting engine rooms on river steamboats. W. & A. Fletcher's engine No. 144 was in good hands.

In the galley behind another wooden bulkhead, Henry Canfield, the Negro cook, diced vegetables and clams to pour over the chunks of bacon sizzling in the huge pots on the range. The chef's knife was almost lost in his big hands as it rocked across the block. Canfield, another of the few veterans aboard, had taken on a nineteen-year-old lad, Edwin Robinson, as his helper. Robinson was engaged in the eternal task saved especially for cooks' assistants, peeling potatoes. Both paused as they heard two bells and a jingle, the signal for half speed astern. The vessel was backing out into the river for the start of the day's trip.

In the engine room, Conklin moved the starting bar of the giant engine. Brandow kept an eye on the gauges and fed water to the condenser. At the signal to stop, the chief engineer brought the ponderous crank of the paddle-wheel shaft to a halt just short of dead center, so that it would not "lock" when reversed. Then one bell sounded — the signal for full speed ahead. Conklin tripped the eccentrics, which operated the steam valves automatically, and the side-wheeler was on her way down the Hudson, headed for the other side of Manhattan.

The *Slocum*'s regular two-trips-a-day route took her *south:* from the Battery at the lower tip of Manhattan, down through the Upper Bay, the Narrows, and the Lower Bay, around Sea Gate on Coney Island and into Rockaway Inlet. But for this excursion trip to Locust Grove on Long Island Sound, she would be steaming *north:* up the East River, past Blackwell's (now Roosevelt) Island, through the strait between Ward's Island and Astoria in Queens (the navigational nightmare called Hell Gate), and out into Long Island Sound.

23

But first the vessel had to stop at the Third Street pier to pick up St. Mark's *Wasserfahrt.*

On the lower East Side the people of Little Germany were already awake. Mothers were up and into their corsets, corset covers, three flannel petticoats, serge skirts, and white shirtwaists with leg-of-mutton sleeves, spinning long braids into intricate chignons. The children were up too, the boys donning double-breasted jackets, long ribbed stockings, knickers, and patent leather shoes; the girls slipping into fancy shirtwaists and skirts or gaily colored sacques, and the most popular female footwear of the day, Oxford ties.

By now the ceremony attending the coronation of the man of the house was under way. Papa, in his natural gray, genuine-wool ribbed union suit, had pulled his long woolen socks well up over the legs of his full-length underwear and slipped into his stiff blue serge trousers. His highly polished heavyweight calfskin bluchers with freshly pressed laces waited by the dresser; he had only to slip into them, pull up the laces, and crisscross them neatly through the hooks atop the shoes. Mama helped him on with his starched shirt and snapped on the fine fifteen-cent linen cuffs he had chosen to wear for this festive day. While Papa struggled to attach the stubborn collar to the shirt by the back button, the front one sprang from his hand, and the family joined in the daily search for the elusive button, hiding this time just behind the front right leg of the dresser.

When the collar was finally in place about Papa's neck, Mama made a knot in the four-in-hand tie and squeezed it between the tabs. Papa lifted his embroidered cross-back suspenders over his shoulders and snapped them in place, then Mama helped him on with his vest and jacket, handed him his correctly blocked derby, and the coronation was completed.

It would reach nearly 80 degrees this day, and the way Papa was dressed, it seemed the idea was to keep the warm air out rather than let the cool air in. Insulation was the thing, not ventilation. Besides, Papa had his own method of cooling the body. He would stop at Frese's Saloon for a few cold lagers on the way to the pier.

Mama kissed him and drank in the exciting fragrance of bay rum on Papa's face. It was best to kiss him now, for after a day of beer, herring, limberger cheese, whiskey, and cigars, he would never smell quite the same. Papa adroitly retrieved the half-finished cigar that had gathered a tongue-stinging flavor on the door lintel overnight, and he was gone.

As Papa left for the saloon, Mama sneaked out a hat she had been saving for this occasion. It was in the new turban style — the Gainsborough Turban. "Hand made on a wire frame covered and draped with handsome imported straw braids," the ad had said. "The trimming, fully to the left, is comprised of four elegant pink crushed roses with full foliage in tinted shades interspersed in the background of roses." Mama mounted this monument to the milliners' art on her head, fastened it firmly with her longest hatpins, and fancied herself a Gibson Girl. The impatient demands of her children soon woke her from reverie. She scooted them out the door, then followed proudly down the hallway stairs.

The streets were filled with a happy throng. Girls bounced down the freshly washed steps of the high stoops, boys rode the wrought-iron banisters to the shiny brass finials at the bottom. The smell of soap and brass polish filled the air. The neighborhood was as clean, fresh, and bright as the faces of the children. At the corner the ever-present German band was splitting the air — a red-eyed, red-nosed trio of round men, who had sallied forth early to boost the festive mood of the excursionists and send the crowd marching happily toward the Third Street pier. They tried to ignore local teen-agers, who liked to eat vinegar pickles under their noses and so cause the musicians' mouths to pucker — a popular prank — but finally they gave up and scurried for the nearest saloon.

The parade that had moved out consisted mostly of women and children. Some men had come along, those who could get away — the older ones in somber suits and derbies to help out at the bars and food stands, the young blades to dazzle the girls with their manly physiques set off by broad-shouldered jackets above extremely tight trousers, tapering down to ankle huggers above two-toned serge and patent leather shoes. From beneath their wide-brimmed straw skimmers, these lady killers eyed the mature female forms, helped out by pinch-waist corsets and hip pads, and then turned to the younger ones, whose dress offered less resistance to the male curiosity. Which of the girls might go *spazieren* (strolling) in the woods at Locust Grove?

Down from Fourteenth and up from Rivington Street, the people came for the seventeenth annual excursion of St. Mark's Evangelical Lutheran Church. From the new borough across the river, Brooklyn, they came by the Grand and Houston Street ferries and the "old" Brooklyn and "new" Williamsburg bridges. From across the Hudson, they arrived by ferry and commuter boats. From the Bronx, they took the Second and Third Avenue Interborough Rapid Transit Elevated Lines. Some, who came by surface transportation, missed the boat, because of a short circuit in the trolley lines or a delay on the horsecars. For most it was a long trip, but the Freses had only to take a fast walk across the Houston Street Ferry Plaza and along the waterfront path that joined Houston with Third Street.

By this time the *General Slocum* was well on its way to this East River pier for its rendezvous with the eager crowd. As she rounded the Battery, a southerly breeze rippled the colored bunting along her sides, snapped up the forty-five star "Old Glory" at the stern, and unfurled a large white banner on the foremast revealing, in large black letters, the name "General Slocum."

26

From the mouth of the East River, the Brooklyn Bridge, the Roeblings' wonder of steel and stone, loomed ahead — a ponderous span ingeniously suspended by a network of what looked like threads. Passing under the bridge, Pilot Van Wart pulled hard to starboard for the first turn in the torturous waterway and passed the towers being erected for the Manhattan Bridge, the third to be thrown across the East River. Following the fairway to Corlears Hook, he then turned the ship toward Brooklyn, where he straightened her out and hugged the shore till he passed the new Williamsburg Bridge. Here he made a wide circle and headed downstream to dock at the end of the Third Street pier. Below, Engineer Conklin responded to the bell-and-jingle code from the wheelhouse, stopping, then reversing the paddle wheels. The water beneath them boiled, seethed, then simmered into silence. The vessel glided to a halt. Hawsers whirred through chocks, pilings creaked as the *General Slocum* was slowly warped to the pier. It was 8:20 A.M.

No sooner had the gangplank touched the pier than policemen Kelk and Van Tassel went aboard to look after the safety of the picnickers. In anticipation of the cry "boy overboard," they took their places on the offside, and none too soon. In a moment a spate of adolescents flooded the decks, seeking favored spots along the rails. The scamps had scooted ahead of the Reverend Mr. George Haas, pastor of St. Mark's, who was now taking his place at the foot of the gangplank to greet his congregation.

A good-natured cheer went up as Professor George Maurer's Band marched aboard to take its place on the cool shady after promenade deck. Then the formal boarding began. As smiling mothers greeted the pastor in German and English, he confided to his wife that he had "worked hard to make this better than any excursion before."

For an hour the stream of men, women, and children poured over the gangplank, filling every spot around the decks. Some were sporting parasols given out by an enterprising salesman as they boarded, lauding the merits of "Steinbugler's Furniture Store" on Avenue A. As the time to sail approached, a querulous hum altered the gay chatter of the crowd. What was the hold-up?

The answer was at the end of the gangplank. Two women were trying to wheedle Pastor Haas into waiting just a few more minutes for their sisters from Brooklyn, who they were *sure* would arrive any minute. The boat stood by for ten minutes longer, then made ready to sail.

As the plank was lifted from the pier, it was discovered that eleven-year-old Johnny Roseman had no ticket. Children were to have free passage, but what was the age limit? It must have been ten, for Johnny was promptly put off.

He was not the last to leave, however. Mrs. Philip Straub of St. Mark's Place had had a premonition, which she had been fighting till the zero hour. After revealing it to a man nearby, she raced toward the plank, calling ahead to hold it. The man, who had evidently found her alarm contagious, followed with his wife and five children. They were the lucky ones.

When the plank was finally pulled in, Deckhand John Coakley held his throbbing head to ease his usual morning headache and checked the mechanical counter in his hand. It read 982. This was not the total number of passengers aboard. The counter was accurate enough, but Coakley had defeated its purpose by clicking it once for every two children under fourteen and once for every adult; then reckoning there were *about* 1,000 aboard.

As a result, the exact number of people aboard the *Slocum* that day will never be known. The best guess, given by the New York City Department of Public Charities in its annual report for 1904, is that 1,331 persons were aboard the vessel, 800 female, the rest male, including the 35-man crew. Of the passengers, more than 500 were under twenty years of age. We will never know how many Coakley misjudged, either as children or as adults; all we do know is that his count was grossly inaccurate.

Finally, at 9:40, the lines were cast off, the pilothouse rang for slow ahead, a tremor, a struggle for movement ran through the vessel, water boiled beneath the giant paddle wheels, children thrilled as the deck's vibration tickled their feet. Then they were off. The band struck up a favorite German hymn, and the people one by one took it up until all were singing what was to be their own requiem: "A mighty fortress is our God, our helper He amid the Flood."

The gleaming white ship moved downstream to come about under the Williamsburg Bridge. As it circled back, Mrs. Charles Pfeifer on the top deck waved to a lone policeman above. From his post on the bridge Sergeant Pfeifer waved back to his bride of a year, and the last plaintive note of the parting hymn drifted back to him with the last wave of his sweetheart's last good-bye.

On the after promenade deck below, Professor George Maurer now lifted his baton and tapped for attention. Awaiting the downbeat, George Dillemuth raised the bow over his beloved violin, Julius Wohl wet the reed on his clarinet, and August Schneider lifted a highly polished trumpet to the ready position. His three children watched as Papa squinched his face to attain the proper embouchure. At the downbeat, the band launched into the German favorite, "*Unser Kaiser Friedrich Marsch*," and the crowd exploded into a festive mood. Girls danced, and boys grinned and grimaced, aping them with awkward attitudes. Mothers bounced lusty babies on their knees to the beat of the stirring march and hummed the familiar tune. Others promenaded on the cool open decks, remarking on the cleanliness of the vessel, an attribute that would warm any German *Hausfrau*'s heart.

Those reading the excursion program were warmed by the

29

words: *"Allen, die heute unsere Gaeste sind bei unserer Siebzehnten Wasserfahrt ein herzliches Wilkommen!"* (A friendly welcome to all our guests on our seventeenth boat trip.) The column next to it gave some interesting news "for everyone who had a stomach." It listed the menu and prices and explained that food would be exchanged for meal tickets, price 5 cents each. Franks and potato salad were fifteen cents, clam chowder twenty, and coffee and cake ten. Featured also were five-cent ham or tongue sandwiches and pie at five cents a portion. The neighborhood merchants aboard checked their ads for proper spelling, lettering, and size, and music lovers turned to page three to find what the next selection by Maurer's Band was to be. Yes, there it was, the "Poet and the Peasant Overture!"

On his rounds Captain William Van Schaick greeted Pastor Haas and his party in the women's cabin, and on his way through the bar savored the heady aroma of clam chowder cooking in the bar kitchen. "Don't give my men too much to drink," he admonished August Lutjens, the volunteer bartender.

"Leave it to me," young Lutjens assured him.

The captain disappeared around the newel post of the forward companionway and mounted the stairs on his way back to his cabin, two decks directly above.

Over the captain's cabin, the highest spot on the vessel, was the pilothouse. Inside, Second Pilot Ed Weaver had been watching the older man at the wheel. First Pilot Edward Van Wart hugged the Brooklyn shore, leaving the Shell Reef buoy well to port. Then he hauled over to the New York side to enter the channel west of Blackwell's Island. When the spindle tower on Man-of-War rock went by to starboard, he brought the vessel into the fairway in the direction of Hell Gate.

Four decks below, the steam steering gear in the forward cabin responded to each movement of the pilothouse wheel. With each hiss and gasp of its pistons the temperature of the little room rose. The tinderbox, created by a thousand acts of negligence, was ready to ignite.

Along the shore, the people waved to the boys and girls dancing about the decks. At Twenty-sixth Street the patients of Bellevue Hospital were transported to happier times for a brief moment, and at Fourty-second the men at the slaughterhouse paused in their sullen trade for a passing glimpse of innocent pleasure. The drab panorama of that part of the city went by on the port side: ferry slips, coal yards, gas tanks, and breweries, while on the other the somber structures of Blackwell's Island passed. Blackwell's was the city's back closet, where it hid away hospitals, insane asylums, penal institutions. In these tombs for the living, patients and inmates listened to the tinkle of laughter and music drifting across the water from another world.

As the vessel slipped into the channel, the pilots exchanged mutual looks of commiseration. Up ahead, at the northern tip of Blackwell's, between Ward's Island and Astoria in Queens County, was Hell Gate, where the waters of Long Island Sound met those of New York Harbor and the East River. The reefs and ripping tides of this channel had battered ships for centuries — indeed, it had been given its sinister name by the Dutch explorer Adriaen Block as long ago as 1614 — and its reputation was infamous among local pilots. Only the night before, the *Chester Chapin* had run aground on Negro Point Reef to avoid hitting another steamer — the latest of a thousand accidents before the *Slocum* entered.

Before it was cleared of its many obstacles, Hell Gate was a raging, roaring tide race filled with rocky reefs and islands with strange, whimsical names: The Bread and Cheese Rocks at the north end of Blackwell's; the middle reef with its Great and Little Mill Rocks, Negro Heads, Hens and Chickens, Gridiron, and Flood Rock. And as if the rocks and reefs were not enough, nature had added two unequal tides, one ebbing and flowing

31

two hours before the other in a pattern of almost perpetual motion.

This was the channel the *Slocum* now had to navigate. Some improvements had been made on nature, and many of the rocks and reefs had been removed. Nevertheless, Hell Gate remained one of the most treacherous straits on the eastern seaboard. Captain Van Schaick would be in to "see her through," but like all pilots, Weaver and Van Wart would be glad when their vessel had safely passed through the moiling strait.

Brushing up his walrus mustache, Van Wart peered from under bushy eyebrows at the water surface before him. He had spent thirty of his sixty-two years as a pilot, and the river surface had few mysteries for him. Riffles revealed shoal water, calm water indicated deeps. With the buoys, spindles, and light-houses now marking the river for navigation, the *Slocum* could hardly go astray.

Still, there were other hazards. Over two dozen ferries cut across the course the *Slocum* was following, and thirty big ships of the Joy, Providence, and Fall River lines used the crowded waterway as a thoroughfare, not to mention ferries, lighters, tugs, and other excursion boats. Van Wart had to keep his mind on what he was doing.

Up on the top deck, a passenger named Charles Lang, a former Coney Island lifeguard, marked off Fifty-fifth Street in his mind by a brewery he recognized on the Manhattan shore. He had just noted it when he overheard a deckhand mutter, "There's something doing forward." He thought he heard the word "fire," but saw no evidence of one. As a precaution he moved his family forward to a less crowded spot, just outside the captain's cabin.

Inside, Captain Van Schaick had been sitting at his desk since the vessel left the Third Street pier. Now the speaking tube roused him: "Captain! Captain Van Schaick! We're coming up on Hell Gate." It was the voice of Ed Weaver.

The captain rose slowly and went to the speaking tube. "I'll be right up, Mr. Weaver." He stepped out on the hurricane deck. It was 9:53. The piers of the new bridge going up at Fifty-ninth Street — the Queensborough — had slipped behind, and the vessel was passing Sixty-fourth Street. The children all about him were cheering for the *Grand Republic*, just passing by. The captain waved, too, then made his way to the pilothouse above, just as Deckhand John Coakley went past with two policemen.

After counting the passengers as they had boarded, Coakley had taken the two officers on a grand tour around the ship. That done, he left them and made his way below for a beer, which the bartender had promised earlier. As he slid down the stairway to the forward main deck saloon, Blackwell's Island lighthouse went by to port. Eighty-sixth Street, he thought as he made for the bar. August Lutjens, the teenage volunteer bartender, greeted him with a big hello and a cool, frothy beer. This was what Coakley liked, beer. It was one of the pleasant fringe benefits that augmented his weekly pay of $6.25. With his work done and a beer in his hands, John Coakley settled down for his free ride to Locust Grove.

Across the water at Broadway on the Astoria shore, John Ronan, a dockworker, looked up from his toil to remark on the gaiety on the passing pleasure boat. "Look at the *Slocum*," he said to a fellow worker. "Don't it make you hate to work when you see a crowd having as good a time as that?" It must be about ten, he thought. It was 9:57.

A minute later the ferryboat *Haarlem*, plying between Ninety-second Street and the Astoria shore, passed under the stern of the *Slocum*. As the paddle wheeler went by, a lone ferryman waved to the children dancing on the afterdecks. One waved back, and soon others joined in a good-natured ovation for the ferryman. The *Slocum* rounded Hallets Point (a headland jutting out from the Astoria side), just north of Blackwell's, and the ferryman saw her no more. At this point workers in a stone yard on Hallets Point noticed a puff of smoke hanging over the vessel, as did the onlookers along the Astoria shore. They thought nothing of it. After all, the band was still playing.

From the other side of the narrow channel, the picture was more somber. People on Ward's Island, another of the "welfare" islands in the East River, saw smoke coming from two forward portholes under the main deck guards, but the three men in the pilothouse were staring intently toward the exit from Hell Gate dead ahead, apparently unaware. Many of the Ward's Island people ran to the shore, waving wildly and pointing to the danger below. The excursionists waved back goodnaturedly, wondering at the curious behavior of the people on shore. Then it occurred to them that they may have been from the "loony house" just three hundred yards away.

As the *General Slocum* eased her way carefully through the narrows of Hell Gate, the music carried up to the Astoria Gas and Light Works at Lawrence Point, the northern tip of Astoria, where Superintendent Grafling noticed smoke coming from the forward part of the approaching vessel.

"That smoke's getting thicker every minute," said one of his crew.

"She's afire!" shouted another.

"With the band still playing?" Grafling grabbed his field glasses and followed the ship through the pass between Astoria and Sunken Meadow, a marshy, uninhabited speck of an island. The burning boat continued on past a dredge off the point, where William Alloway, the operator, saw a burst of flame forward. He blew four blasts on the dredge whistle to alert the pilots, but the *Slocum* kept going. It was 10:05 by his engine-room clock. He looked up again to watch the boat steam away. Suddenly, in the middle of a popular tune, the band stopped playing. The boat exploded into flame.

THE LOST MOMENTS

As DECKHAND JOHN Coakley skipped down the stairs into the main deck saloon for his "first for the day," Blackwell's Island Lighthouse was to starboard of the *Slocum* and the East River (now Carl Schurz) Park to port. The boat was passing Eighty-sixth Street.

Above, in the pilothouse, First Pilot Van Wart was making ready for the difficult maneuver of entering the narrows of Hell Gate. Captain Van Schaick, who had come in to see the vessel through, as was the custom, watched with Second Pilot Ed Weaver as the pilot nosed the *Slocum* into the first move of the giant S turn. A long blast from the ferryboat *Haarlem* told them that she had just left her slip at Ninety-second Street, bound for the Astoria shore. The distance to the ferry and the swiftness of the sleek excursion boat ruled out any fear of collision. The ferry would merely cross the *Slocum*'s wake. Van

Wart pulled hard astarboard, and the side-wheeler's double wake swept across the bow of the ferry. As it did, the last wreath of foam circled the lips of the thirsty deckhand, and a wide-eyed boy came running up to him and cried:

9:59   "Mister, there's smoke coming up one of the stairways." Coakley screwed up his young but tired face and summoned up all the experience of his eighteen days aboard to meet the emergency. Reluctantly he put down his glass and walked the twenty-five feet to the entrance of the cabin below. Smoke was seeping through a chink in the door; as he slid the panel back, a stream of it streaked out on a current of air. Coakley waved aside the smoke, then ran his hand across his brow to help him think. Then, with the same faulty reasoning that had led him to miscount the passengers, he ignored the pilothouse blower on the doorjamb beside him and stepped down the narrow stairway to the cabin entrance below. He then did what no one should ever do when fire is suspected in the next room. He opened the door.

In the forward cabin, the smoldering hay in the barrels, hungry for air, burst into open flame. Coakley stood gaping.

10:00   The smoke was sucked up by the updraft to the deck above, and from there it streamed past the knot of people who were awaiting Coakley's return, then up the companionway and through the airy promenades and cabins. At each point along the way its presence was interpreted differently. The Webers on the upper deck laughed it off as "clam chowder boiling over." Others dismissed it as clams frying or the smell of a relighted cigar. Only little Lillie Mannheimer hit upon the awful truth. "I think the boat's on fire," she said and was admonished by her aunt about creating a riot.

Another stream of smoke, seen only by the people on the Ward's Island shore, was pouring from the portholes and running back under the guards and up into the air at the stern to form a cloud over the vessel. A man on the fantail noting this, went forward to investigate. He later remembered the boat was passing a marble yard he knew on Hallets Point at the time.

By now, to the formation of curious passengers at the forward-cabin entrance came several people who would do more than watch. Twelve-year-old Frank Perditsky ran off to spread the alarm. John Engelman, a veteran tugboatman, who knew Hell Gate well and was aware what a fire aboard such a vessel meant, waited for Coakley to reappear and, when he did not, decided to act. He took his wife Louisa and six-year-old son out onto the starboard walk and gauged the distance to the Astoria shore. It did not seem far, and he *was* a strong swimmer. Why not? He helped his family over the outside rail, scaled it himself, and leaped into the tide race. With his wife and son clinging to him, Engelman set out for the rocky mainland. But the raging current, which was pushing the *Slocum* to its doom, was too powerful for him. It tore the boy away. The bereaved mother's tears were lost in the waters of Hell Gate, her cries in the music still playing up above.

10:01

Into the insular world of the pilothouse not even a hint of trouble had penetrated. Pilot Van Wart had maneuvered the boat around Hallets Point and was having a devil of a time straightening out the yawing vessel, which was being forced toward the Astoria shore, when the captain noticed a rather grim face in the jolly crowd on the deck below. It was little Frank Perditsky. From where he stood, Frankie could see only the grave face and white mustache beneath the gold-trimmed cap marked "Captain" and assumed that he alone was taking the boat through. Awed by such a tower of authority, Frankie hesitated for a moment. Then he mustered his courage and shouted, "Hey, mister, the ship's on fire!"

Used to such pranks from mischievous kids, the captain scared him off with "Get the hell out of here and mind your own business," then turned back to the serious work of getting his boat through the gate. Van Wart, still at the wheel, read the

37

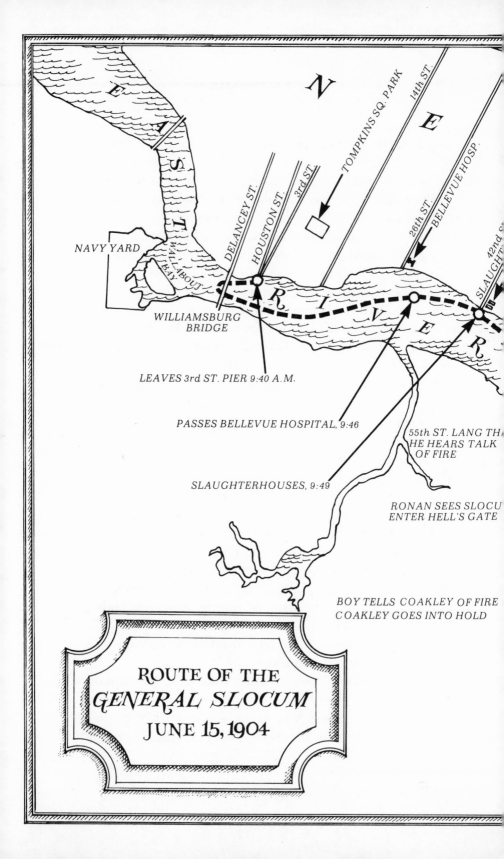

NAVY YARD

WILLIAMSBURG
BRIDGE

LEAVES 3rd ST. PIER 9:40 A.M.

PASSES BELLEVUE HOSPITAL, 9:46

SLAUGHTERHOUSES, 9:49

55th ST. LANG TH.
HE HEARS TALK
OF FIRE

RONAN SEES SLOCU
ENTER HELL'S GATE

BOY TELLS COAKLEY OF FIRE
COAKLEY GOES INTO HOLD

ROUTE OF THE
GENERAL SLOCUM
JUNE 15, 1904

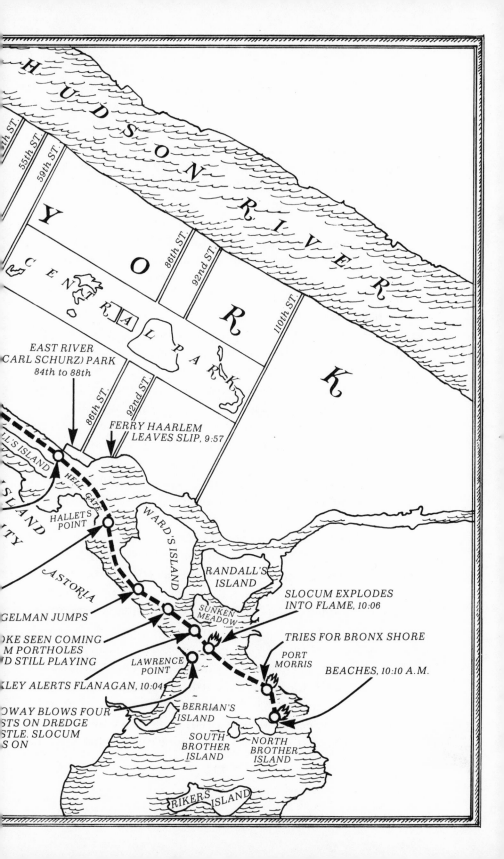

HUDSON RIVER

NEW YORK

55th ST.
59th ST.
86th ST.
92nd ST.
110th ST.

CENTRAL PARK

EAST RIVER
(CARL SCHURZ) PARK
84th to 88th

86th ST.
92nd ST.

FERRY HAARLEM
LEAVES SLIP, 9:57

ELL'S ISLAND

HELL GATE

HALLET'S
POINT

WARD'S
ISLAND

RANDALL'S
ISLAND

ASTORIA

GELMAN JUMPS

OKE SEEN COMING
M PORTHOLES
D STILL PLAYING

SUNKEN
MEADOW

LAWRENCE
POINT

KLEY ALERTS FLANAGAN, 10:04

OWAY BLOWS FOUR
STS ON DREDGE
STLE. SLOCUM
S ON

BERRIAN'S
ISLAND

SOUTH
BROTHER
ISLAND

SLOCUM EXPLODES
INTO FLAME, 10:06

TRIES FOR BRONX SHORE

PORT
MORRIS

BEACHES, 10:10 A.M.

NORTH
BROTHER
ISLAND

RIKERS ISLAND

surface pattern up ahead: rough over Middle Reef, smooth over the fourteen-fathom channels on either side. The *Slocum* was now hitting a good fifteen miles an hour, with a strong tail current driving her toward the rocks. The three minds in the pilothouse now had but one thought: getting out of these damned waters! But how? By which channel?

10:03   Three decks below, a smaller mind had a larger problem. John Coakley had been in the forward cabin belowdecks for three minutes now, groping about for something with which to dampen the growing fire.

He had tried to throw a folded tarpaulin over the flames, but it was tied down. Then, hoping to smother the fire at least temporarily, he grabbed the nearest things at hand — two bags of charcoal. Reasoning that they would do the job for the time being, he threw them over the fire, then scrambled up the steps to find help. On the deck above, the goggling crowd about the door blocked his way, asking for a verdict on the fate of the ship. Coakley, though badly shaken, said nothing, as he shouldered his way through to look aft in the long cabin. Not a crewman was in sight. He slid open the starboard door and looked up and down the deck, then ran around to the port side and aft.

10:04   By now the men above had decided on the northern channel out. Van Wart brought the vessel over to port between Middle Ground Reef and the cool green slough of Sunken Meadow. The black channel buoy went by to starboard, as it should have "going out." All had gone well for them. Hell Gate was past.

Below, Coakley's mind had settled on the idea of passing the buck to some higher authority, and so the object of his search became ship's officer Ed Flanagan, an ex-ironworker, who had assumed the title "First Mate" without the benefit of a mate's license. Flanagan was at the forward port gangway with Porter Payne, watching Deckhand O'Neill and another officer of dubious rank, "Second Mate" Corcoran, lay out a new line.

At the sight of the excited Coakley, Flanagan held up his

hand to calm him lest he alarm the passengers. As Sunken Meadow was going by, Coakley broke into the circle, grabbed Flanagan by the arm, and whispered hoarsely, "Mate, the ship's afire forward, and it's making pretty good headway."

Flanagan's heavy jaw dropped lower than usual, and a more **10:05** vapid look came over his already dull face. Lumbering forward, his awkward squad behind, he entered the main deck saloon. The smoke was thicker than ever. Elbowing his way through the mob, he looked down into the fiery hold. Now his lack of experience caught up with him. Here he was with over a thousand passengers aboard a burning ship and a crew of worthless landlubbers he had scraped from New York's waterfront. It was his turn to seek some higher authority.

In the engine room, Chief Engineer Ben Conklin was yelling to his assistant, Everett Brandow, about the smoothness of the engines when the thick frame of Flanagan filled the doorway. "Chief, the ship's afire forward," the mate almost pleaded. Conklin, who had been with the *Slocum* from the start, eyed the mountain of confusion before him. Was it possible this man did not know what to do? Conklin told him to alert the pilothouse and take down the hose, thoughts that apparently had never occurred to the "first mate."

Flanagan ran forward as fast as his clumsy hulk would allow and did what Coakley should have done six minutes before: He yelled up the blower, "The ship's afire forward!" Then, going **10:06** back to the forward standpipe, he jumped up to loosen the fire hose from the rack, almost out of reach.

It came down coil and all onto the deck. He pulled the nozzle from the center and handed it to Tom Collins, a veteran of four days aboard the *Slocum*. As Collins ran to the door of the cabin stairway, not thirty feet away, the hose twisted like a party streamer and kinked in a dozen places. Someone hollered, "Turn on the water!"

Conklin, at the donkey engine, was doing just that, for al-

41

though the water had always been "on" in the sanitary lines for the water closets and sinks, it had never been fed through the fire lines, since they were never used or tested. As the valve opened, the water rushed to the forward standpipe and into the hose. The kinked fire hose writhed and kicked like a wounded snake. The passengers and crew lined up along its length to subdue the unruly beast, but it was no use. A few drops dripped from the nozzle, the rotten hose burst, then the coupling flew off the standpipe, and the crew broke up and scattered.

Payne the porter made a vain attempt to connect a rubber hose. The coupling did not fit. Flanagan took over, botched the job too, then mumbled something like "Get to the boats," and disappeared. Corcoran and Payne went back to the door of the forward cabin and babbled about which one of them should go down; Payne volunteered. As he dropped into the hold, a cloud of smoke belched from the room, then flames. Payne slid the door shut, but it was too late. The fire ate away the flimsy frame and followed Payne up the narrow stairway.

Someone yelled, *"Fire!"* and the panic was on.

Second Pilot Weaver had just noticed the spindle buoy off Sunken Meadow go by and was watching Van Wart get ready for the wide swing around Lawrence Point when the isolation of the bridge was shattered by the words most dreaded aboard **10:06** ship: *"The ship's on fire!"*

No kid's prank this time. That was unmistakably the voice of Flanagan.

This terrifying phrase froze the three men at their posts for a few seconds, then the captain gulped, "I'll go down and see about it." He slid back the door, looked out, and blanched at the sight. A sheet of flame had come up over the port side, and a breeze across the bow was whipping it back over the freshly painted upper works.

The stunned captain, who had carried over 30 million people safely to their destinations, could hardly believe the scene was real. Screaming passengers stampeded to the stern. Women and children were going over the side. The band suddenly stopped playing. Smoke was everywhere, and even above the bedlam he could hear the ominous crackle of the advancing flames.

He slammed the door. His wooden ship was doomed. His experience with river fires told him that much. The only question now was where to land. Hell Gate was behind him.* Even Sunken Meadow had gone by astern, and with the current running so strong, it would be impossible to swing the boat around. If the steering gear broke, the vessel would broach and be drawn into the middle of the river.

In his highly confused state, he blurted out, "Put her on North Brother Island!" At this, Van Wart signaled for full speed ahead and rang the fire gongs on the decks. Weaver blasted away on the boat's whistle, and the *General Slocum* broke out into the Bay of Brothers.

10:07

The mad race for the island, three minutes away, was on.

---

*William Van Schaick has been criticized by writers for three quarters of a century for not having landed the vessel while it was in Hell Gate — that is, as soon as the smoke was first sighted. This idea is based on the mistaken reports of contemporary newspaper and magazine writers, who assumed that the captain knew of the fire as soon as it was discovered.

In fact, Coakley did not report the fire immediately but wasted precious minutes going below. In this crucial early period, while the fire was taking hold, smoke and flame were carried away from the pilothouse by the motion of the ship. Thus the *Slocum* was allowed to proceed through Hell Gate and into the approaches to the Sound before Van Schaick was notified of what was happening to his vessel. By the time Flanagan reported to him, the *Slocum* had little choice of landing site.

Van Schaick had his shortcomings, but they were not navigational.

PANDEMONIUM

THE FLAMES WERE on their way now, racing through the boat without a metal door or bulkhead to stay them. Upward and aft a strong vengeful wind carried the hot fumes and fire through the once cool promenades and cabins, turning the carefree crowd of a few minutes before into a pack of maddened creatures scrambling for safety. Each person, shocked into action by a scream or the horror of the fire itself leaping into view, made his own frantic effort to escape. Some went over the side immediately. Others, hypnotized by the sight of the fire, stood in frozen panic. Those crushed to the wall were fried by sizzling white paint. Women, their bulky clothes fuel for the fire, ran like screaming human torches through the mob of crazed people. The primitive urge to climb up and away from danger took over and companionways were soon jammed with fighting, shouting passengers.

Pastor Haas, who had left the women's cabin aft to see to his flock, had been graciously greeted as he passed through the promenade saloon above. As he stepped out on the open deck forward, he noticed smoke coming up the companionway ahead. Like others he thought of the clam chowder in the main-deck kitchen below, but at the head of the stairs, the smoke grew thicker, and as he descended, a burst of flame appeared. Reentering the promenade saloon, he drove the people of his congregation aft away from the fire.

A few seconds later, or so it seemed, the pastor looked back and saw that the advancing flames had already reached the cabin and were racing toward him along the walls of polished wood. Red velvet and wickerwork went up like a haystack in a parched field.

He fought his way back down to the women's cabin and there tried to calm the wild mob that had taken refuge within its flimsy walls. Screaming women and children were running blindly about, seeking safety anywhere. The pastor tried to slam the door on the oncoming fire, but the door jammed, and the relentless flames crept in.

Anna Frese, the little pianist from Mangin Street, had stayed forward near the main-deck bar with her family and friends. "We were talking of the good times we were going to have at the Grove," she recalled later. When they saw the smoke, they walked over to get a closer look. "Three of the crew were talking — who would go down to see what was burning? No sooner did one go down and open the door than a big flame came out, and he could not shut the door again. So the fire had a good chance to go right up the stairs to the upper decks."

The fire roared into the saloon, and people began to stampede aft. Anna saw the mate giving orders to get the hose, but the crew seemed to be doing little else to put out the fire. "By that time, the fire had made great headway up the stairs, and I heard chairs falling and people calling out for their children.

45

They started to close the front doors, which separated us [in the forward section, where the fire had started] from the rest of the boat. We were the only ones out there, my father, the three girls, and myself."

Mr. Frese, seeing no help from the cowardly and incompetent crew, took the four girls outside, helped them over the rail, and told them to hang on until he gave them the signal to jump. They waited.

Amidships, John Halphausen, sexton of St. Mark's Church, saw the excitement from another angle. When the crew went berserk and passengers rampaged, he took refuge behind the starboard paddle-box housing with his two daughters, and from there, in the wings, watched one of the many mad scenes being enacted at that time on the *General Slocum*. The mob rushed about, the crew among them, all scurrying for safety in any form. Second Mate Corcoran attempted to mount the stairs to the promenade deck, but a hundred clawing hands pulled him down. First Mate Flanagan, a lost lummox, floundered his way aft, and Coakley, bewildered as ever, strained to reach the life preservers overhead.

Corcoran, escaping from the angry mob at the companion-way, soon joined him and other pitiful suppliants, reaching for their only hope of salvation. The wire mesh holding the preservers to the carlings, jagged and rusty, cut into their hands, but at last it gave way.

Wails of dismay rose from the pleading mass of humanity. The preservers, which had rotted in the racks for thirteen years, fell on the passengers' heads and burst in a shower of powdered cork.

Blinded and choked by cork dust, some maddened passengers abandoned hope and jumped overboard without life belts. Others stayed to fight for the useless things that crumbled in their clutches.

The life jackets still intact were donned by a hopeful few, but some jackets burst upon hitting the water, and the sturdier ones, surviving the impact, became waterlogged and dragged their victims under.

The vessel itself trembled with the frightened people aboard. The walking beam almost leaped from its cradle atop the gallows frame, shaking the ship from keel to masthead. The convulsions of the giant machinery shook the main deck like an earthquake. Windows rattled, deck chairs danced macabrely, and empty fire pails clattered derisively at the screaming, burning people running through a hailstorm of pebbled cork. The upper decks, perched on quivering stanchions, swayed with each movement of the ship, and the pilothouse atop them was fast becoming as unhinged as the man within.

The confused captain was giving conflicting orders to the engine room. Every five seconds jingles, bells, and combinations of both demanded: *Full speed! Stop! Go ahead! Slow! Full speed!* Assistant Engineer Brandow was kept jumping. For a moment the captain considered the Bronx shore. That was it, the Bronx shore! Van Wart pulled to port, but wait — the rocks. . . . the lumber yards . . . the naphtha boats . . . no, better not. For a few seconds the shaky old man pulled himself together.

"Ed, it's all over with her, we can't save her. Keep her jacked up and beach her on North Brother Island right ahead, starboard side in, so the people can jump into shallow water."

With this, Captain William Van Schaick, master pilot and expert handler of side-wheelers, made his last and certainly his most sensible decision as commander of the *General Slocum*. For among the many yards along the Bronx shore was that of the Sileck Lumber Company and, behind it, the tanks of the Central Gas and Light. A flaming vessel, running ashore there, could cause an explosion that might set the whole South Bronx afire.

47

Van Wart turned the flaming arrow away from the Bronx shore and aimed it at the bleak island in the bay.

This sudden erratic maneuver caused havoc at the stern, where the maddened crowd was whipped from side to side by the yawing motion. On the middle deck, by far the most crowded, the passengers had rushed to port, the side nearest the shore, as though pleading with the helpless spectators along the waterfront. The swing of the bow to port pressed them against the rail just long enough for it to give way, and a shrieking mass of humanity was slung overboard. Those who escaped this disaster were sent reeling across the deck to the starboard rail and were slammed against it. This rail snapped too, and another torrent of bodies cascaded into the deep.

The landing place chosen was just off the starboard bow, seven hundred yards, one hundred seconds away — a rocky, unfriendly bit of ground submerged in a few feet of dark churning water. Getting the *Slocum* in would be difficult.

A long pier jutted out from the eastern shore of North Brother Island, making it impossible to beach the vessel, starboard side on, at the shallowest part. Van Wart had to bring the *Slocum* in at an angle, past the pier, then pull hard aport and take a chance on the ship's careening when she struck the hard ground side on. At a closer look, he saw that it would be even more difficult than he had thought. The beach, if it could be called that, was nothing but a patch of cinders at the water's edge, in a cove between the pier and an eight-foot retaining wall.

The island came up big and fast to starboard. As the pier went by, Van Wart turned the bow away from the shore, praying that the boat would come around side on to the beach and not strike the retaining wall ahead. The heat of the fire eating at his face, Van Wart brought the vessel in — but not quite as he wished. The *General Slocum*, recalcitrant to the last, groaned over the island's rocky ledge and slammed to a stop twenty-five feet short of the wall — bow in, stern out, at an angle to the shore.

As the vessel ground to a halt, the three men jumped from the pilothouse to the deck below and ran to the bow. Weaver went over the port rail. Van Wart yelled to the captain to jump — the old man was in a daze. Van Wart yelled again, then crossed himself and went over the starboard side. Van Schaick, his hat afire, followed.

George Heinz, then seventeen, long remembered the scene that day on the forward hurricane deck. He was standing by the lifeboats and noted that no attempt was made to launch one. The crew ran about like madmen, giving no heed to the captain's commands. As he told it later:

"When the panic started, all the people employed on the steamer dived overboard. As far as I could see, at any rate, they didn't go around saying, 'There is no danger. Keep your heads,' the way they do in a book. They just quit."

Young Heinz stood by the rail, entreating the crowd to give the women and children a chance for safety. As he looked around for his family, he saw a little girl kneeling in prayer. He started toward her, but before he could reach her, she went up in flames.

"I was swept over the side. Just before I went, I saw a woman running toward me with her whole head burning. I will never forget it."

Finding himself in the water, he struck out for North Brother Island, fifty yards away. "It seemed an awful long swim with one's clothes on," he said. "I saw a little girl, six or seven, floating near me. The poor little kid's eyes were staring from her head and she was calling for her mama. I made a grab for her and tried to hold her, but the current was so strong I had to let go. I shall never forget it. Men on the island pulled me out of the water with a garden rake. My mother, brother, and two sisters are missing. I guess they're dead."

Fortunately George's guess was not entirely correct; he later found his twelve-year-old brother alive but struck dumb with fright.

Fifty-seven-year-old Nicholas Balzer, too, was trapped forward. He had taken little Freddy Fickbaum up to the top deck to show him some points of interest.

"We were approaching the island," he said later, "when, looking forward, I saw flames shooting up from the deck below. Unclasping my knife, I slashed at the fastenings of the life rafts nearby, but they were secured by wire instead of rope. I told Freddy to stay with me, but when I returned, he had disappeared. I then started for my party, but was driven back by the flames."

By this time the whole front part of the boat was a mass of fire. For the moment, since the *Slocum* was so near to shore, there was no panic. The passengers, mostly women and children, retreated before the flames.

"Everyone thought the boat would put into shore at once," Balzer said, "but it seemed fully five minutes or more before she swung in. By then, the scene was terrifying. Women threw their children overboard and followed them. They had no other refuge from the flames, which swept everything before them. I rushed aft, calling to my wife, but I could not see her, and in the roar of the fire and the cries of the panic-stricken passengers she could not hear me. I was driven back to the wheelhouse by the fire. I thought I was trapped. There was no chance to go farther aft, and the fire was directly below. I climbed down from deck to deck and into the water and swam ashore. The water only came to my armpits — I could have walked it. When I finally emerged, I looked back, and to my dying day I'll never forget the scene."

Around Balzer were a score of bodies, most of them charred

50

and burned. From the stern of the vessel, where hundreds of persons were huddled, fighting like mad to leap into the water, he saw dozens of women with babies in their arms throw themselves over the side.

"I helped as many of the living as possible," he said. He looked in vain for his wife among the living, but she had gone, like so many others, to a watery grave.

Emile Bohmer, a lad of eighteen, was another who tried to use the safety equipment. He rushed to the fire pails, which were half filled with water, and threw the contents of several on the flames, without effect. Then he tried to let down a lifeboat, but found it strapped down tightly and stuck to the deck with paint, so that it could not be moved before the flames drove him away. Bohmer's heroics having proved futile, he jumped overboard, swam about for a few seconds, then picked up a young girl floundering in the water, swam to the nearby paddle wheel, and clung to it till picked up by a tug.

Mrs. Annie Weber was another who attempted to use the *Slocum*'s "safety equipment."

Mrs. Weber was one of a party of five adults and five children: the Webers and their young son and daughter; Mrs. Weber's sister; and her brother, Paul Liebenow, and his wife and their three little ones. "We went on board laughing and talking, the children romping ahead with my sister," she reported later. "We went to the middle deck near the forward part of the boat. The sun was shining, and the boat glided through the water so smoothly that the children could play without danger. . . . We were sitting in a circle talking when a puff of black smoke came up the stairway leading to the deck below. It was a big puff and startled everyone. 'Don't mind that, it's the chowder cooking,' someone said, and then we laughed at our fears, but the laughing changed to a cry of horror when a sheet of flame followed the smoke."

Mrs. Weber called her children, while her sister-in-law ran, carrying her infant, to look for her own two toddlers. When the Weber children failed to appear, the father rushed off hunting for them. "The flames kept sweeping up in puffs, each one growing higher and spreading. . . . We were all separated. I rushed here and there, looking for my children and saying to myself that my husband must have found them."

As the boat raced on, the flames kept sweeping back, and it was like a breath of red-hot furnace. "Get a life preserver!" someone shouted, and Mrs. Weber and others around her stood up on camp stools and benches and reached for the life belts overhead.

"Some of them we could not budge, and others pulled to pieces and spilled the crumbs of cork all over our heads. The heat was blistering, and the flames swept along the roof of the deck and scorched our fingers as we tried to snatch down the life preservers. The flames drove [many people] back and over the side of the boat. Nobody could live in such heat as that. My face was scorching, and my hair caught fire."

Mrs. Weber went to the side of the boat and swung herself over the side by a rope. Every time her hands, face, or body came in contact with the side of the vessel, the hot surface would blister her flesh. "Drop or burn to death," someone cried to her.

"I don't know whether I dropped or whether I was pushed off," she recalled later. "I found myself struggling against the water, and it was hot. Others . . . were in the water all around me, and they were pulling each other down."

She cried out for help and was answered by a nearby swimmer: "You'll have to come over here. The water's too hot where you are."

"I think I must have caught a rope," she concluded. "I was pulled to shore on North Brother Island, and then went back into the water to look for my children."

Mr. Weber, who had run up to the top deck to fetch the children, recalled, "The flames seemed to follow me. I could not find [the children.] It was useless . . . to look, for the flames were all over the boat. No one could live. With the other men I tried to lower a lifeboat. We could manage the rope, but found that the boat was fastened on by wire and could not be lowered. The life preservers were useless — a handful of sawdust."

The two Weber children disappeared in the fire along with their cousins and young aunt. Paul Liebenow went aft till stopped by the blazing interior near the paddle box. He tore at the overhead wire holding the life belts. But what was the use? His family was gone, his friends, everyone. With his hand bleeding and his hair afire, he somehow managed to get to the rail and went over. He was to learn later that his wife had covered the face of their baby, Adelia, jumped over with her clothes afire, and had been picked up by the tug *Franklin Edson*.

Through the long harrowing minutes since the fire broke out of the tinderbox below, Anna Frese, the budding pianist from Mangin Street, had held on to the rail on the main deck waiting for her father's signal to jump. Her recollections of that terrible day were still vivid sixty-four years later:

"Somehow the other girls disappeared. I held on to the railing with my right hand as long as I could, and as the boat went on the rocks, the whole top of the boat crashed into the hulk. My father told me to jump, but I could not get my hand off — it was baked on the rail with the paint."

She managed to wrench herself free, however, and leaped. "I had to be careful to clear the paddle wheel, as people were being caught [in it] and died; so, I tried to jump out far enough, and I struck a rock and broke all my front teeth. I did not realize I was burned so bad till I tried to brush my hair away from my eyes." Later the doctor at the hospital wanted to amputate Anna's arm, but her mother would not hear of it. "My one hope was to become a concert pianist," she said. "But it was two years before I had the bandage and brace off — two years before I could use my hand. My concert days were over."

Anna, like most of those trapped forward, had jumped into shallow water and struggled up onto the beach with the help of friends, relatives, or rescuers from the island. Those farther aft were not so fortunate. The peculiar position of the *Slocum*, beached at an angle, meant that the boat jutted out into the deeper water beyond the island's shelf. It was like a giant fiery pier, a wall of flame cutting off access to land. For those at the wrong end, it was jump or burn, sink or swim.

On the top afterdeck, however, the passengers had been allowed one advantage over those on the lower decks. The enclosures beneath the seats along the rails were filled with the only good life belts aboard the vessel. These life preservers made escape relatively simple. Sixteen-year-old Louise Gailing was one of those who discovered them. She merely strapped the baby she was minding to her back with one of the belts, jumped overboard with her *papoose*, and swam to a nearby tug.

Lucy Hencken had a harder time of it. The fifteen-year-old girl had taken her mother to the top deck for a breath of air and had seated her in a corner behind the paddle-box housing when the fire swept aft.

"My brother was on one of the lower decks," she recalled later. "As soon as we saw the smoke and heard the cries of 'Fire,' my mother asked me to go below and find my brother. When I got down the stairway, I found the crushed bodies of three little babies, who had been trampled on in the terrible scramble. They were all still living, and I carried them up to my mother and put them on her lap. Then I went below to find my brother."

Lucy saw him for a moment, and then he was swept away in a surge of men and women who were rushing from the flames. She succeeded in getting back to the upper deck, but when she

54

went to look for her mother and the three babies, they were gone. "With my mother and brother gone from me, I didn't want to live any longer, so I jumped in. As I was going down, a man on a tugboat caught me with a boat hook and dragged me up on deck."

Fred Hoffman, a twenty-four-year-old fireman from the Bronx, was on the upper deck too with his family. "Little Edna, my brother's three-year-old, was in my arms. [There] were my mother . . . my brother's wife Cecelia, her little boy Raymond, and Jane Workman, my friend. . . . I don't remember much about the fire. It seemed to come from below. I grabbed the boy and called on the women to follow me. First the women were separated from me, and then the crowd swept me and the little ones toward the stern of the boat." In trying to reach the womenfolk of his family he got lost in the crowd and went overboard with it. "I remember nothing but being trampled upon. When I came to the surface, a life preserver was in my reach, and I clung to that. My strength was gone, and it seemed as if I could not hold on a bit longer, when someone pulled me out of the water and took me ashore."

What Fred Hoffman didn't know was that he had gone over with the mob when the top deck had fallen. William Vassner remembered that he *almost* did.

"I was on the top deck when someone shouted, 'Fire.' Everyone tried to jump, and I tried to jump too, but there were so many ahead of me that I couldn't — I kept getting pushed back from the railing. So I grabbed a post. Just then, the deck caved in, and people went crashing down with it. It was an awful sight, a big pile of heads, legs, arms — like a football game, only a thousand times worse."

He clung to the pole for about two minutes and then jumped into the water. Unlike most victims, Vassner could swim, "as well as anyone on the East Side."

"I swam around five different tugs, but they were filled with

55

women and children who couldn't swim. I helped three little fellows to board, and then, getting tired, I swam toward a launch that had only a few on it. I had to push bodies out of my way to reach it. A very large stout woman grabbed me and pulled me under water. When I came up, I was pulled aboard the launch. So was the big woman."

If things were bad on the top afterdeck, they were worse on the promenade deck below, for here those who had tried to climb to the open air above had been caught in the stampede and driven aft into a corral of fire packed to suffocation with hysterical humans. Among those engulfed by the horde were the members of the band and the little children who had been summoned there for refreshments.

Thirteen-year-old John Ell recalled that, as the vessel neared Hell Gate, the children were called down to the lower deck, where ice cream and soda were being served. The youngsters were falling all over each other in their eagerness to get to the tables, so he, his mother, and little brother Paul went to the engine room door to watch the machinery.

"Suddenly and without the least warning there was a burst of flames from the furnace room," he said. "[It] rushed up through the engine room and flashed about us. The flames spread quickly, setting fire to the clothes of the women and children who were [nearby]. . . . There was the most terrible panic as the burning women and children rushed out among those surrounding the ice-cream and soda-water tables, screaming with pain."

At that instant the swing toward the Bronx shore was made. John Ell tried to break through the mad crush and get to his mother and little brother. "But I was swept into one corner of the boat and held there, unable to move. They were swept overboard by the crush against the rail. At one time it seemed as if women and children were pouring over the sides like a waterfall."

As they made for the island shore, the captain blew his whistle in one continuous blast, and soon boats of all descriptions were making for the *Slocum* from every direction. Ell was rescued by a launch just as the boat settled close to the shore.

The love of music had brought Mrs. Catherine Kassebaum and her party to the cool, shady afterdeck. They were gathered not more than twenty feet away from the band and close to the rail.

"The first intimation we had that there was something wrong was a piercing scream . . . from the forward part of the boat. We concluded that someone must have fallen overboard and began scanning the water in the wake of the boat."

Soon there was a general panic on the forward decks. They could hear the women and children screaming, and an instant later there was a puff of smoke and flame near the bow of the boat that told the story. "The moment I saw the flames," Mrs. Kassebaum said later, "I called our party together and told them quietly that, if we were to escape alive, we must all stick close together so as to be able to help one another. I thought the strong among us might be able to save the weak. But my words of warning were no more than out of my mouth when there came such a rush of panic-stricken and frenzied people to the stern of the boat that no human being could have stood up against it."

Mrs. Kassebaum clung to the rail with all her strength and managed to hold her place, but when she looked around, not one of her family was to be seen. "They had been whisked away from me in a mad rush and I did not know what had been their fate. By that time there were scores of women and children in the water, who had jumped overboard to escape the worse fate of being roasted on the boat."

At last she managed to get a foot on the rail. From this point of vantage, she searched the maddened crowd for her vanished family — in vain. She did catch sight of Pastor Haas, however, with his wife and daughter down on the main deck.

"That seemed to give me an idea of my own peril, and I knew that if I expected to escape alive, I must decide on some course quickly. I took another careful look around to see if any of my family were on the boat, but still they were nowhere to be seen. Then I decided to take my chances in the water. Even then the fire was so near me that my face and hands were scorched and blistered, and there were holes in my clothing that had been burned by the flying sparks."

The intrepid woman climbed over the rail and jumped feet first into the water. "It seemed to me that I sank hundreds of feet and that I should never come to the surface again, but at last, I saw a flash of light, and that told me I was up where I could get a breath of air. I tried to keep myself from sinking again by striking out blindly with my hands and feet, and did manage to keep up for a few seconds."

In that brief time, she saw scores of women and little children all about her in the water. They all seemed to be drowning. She wondered, in a dreamy sort of way, if any of them could be her own children. Then her strength failed, and she sank once more.

"That time I thought I should never see the light again. It seemed like an eternity to me. I stopped struggling and didn't seem to care any longer whether I ever rose to the top or not. Just then my head struck against something hard. That aroused my flagging senses, and I grabbed intuitively at whatever had bumped my head . . . and held on."

When her head cleared, and she could breathe again, she discovered that she was clinging to the paddle box. "I held on desperately, and a minute or two later a man in a small boat pulled close to me. The boatman held out an oar and yelled to me to grasp it and hold fast. I did so, and he soon hauled me aboard his boat. I begged him to look for the other members of my family, but he had as many in his boat as it would hold and had to go ashore."

Of a party of eleven three escaped. Mr. Kassebaum came out uninjured, Mrs. Kassebaum was badly burned, and one of her two married daughters, Annette — who had run to the top deck and jumped onto a tug — suffered a broken leg in the fall.

The entire band had not been, as many thought, pushed overboard at once. It had played while the fire smoldered in the forward cabin, while Coakley bungled about below. It was playing when Flanagan yelled the alarm up the signal pipe, and it was still playing when the rushing tide of desperate people swept half of it away.

William Zimmerman, John Buhl, and "Ikey," the drummer boy, had gone over with Julius Wohl and his clarinet. The others had been permitted a minute longer in the fight for survival.

Professor George Maurer, the bandmaster, adroitly side-stepped the rush, then threw down his baton and told his wife and three daughters to follow him. He rushed up to the nearest place where life belts were stowed. There, belt after belt was pulled down from the carlings above, all rotten. The bandmaster paused to think. Perhaps it was only these life belts that were no good. He told his oldest daughter to try near the paddle box, where the *good* life belts might be. Then he took his wife and two younger daughters to the rail. He found a rope hanging offside and told his wife to slide down, then took the frightened girls, one by each hand. Together, the three of them jumped.

Mrs. Maurer saw them hit the water safely but a man came hurtling down toward them feet first. Later a heel mark on Maurer's head told the story: he had died of concussion and dragged his daughters to their deaths.

Ten days later, after fighting pneumonia brought on by shock and exposure, Mrs. Maurer succumbed, too. Only the

Maurers' oldest daughter, Mrs. Charles Gemin, survived. Apparently she had found a *good* life belt somewhere.

August Schneider, cornetist, and his family were allowed to stay with the *Slocum* a little longer — till she was beached. The turn toward the island had shifted the course of the wind, then running almost stem to stern, to one across the beam, port to starboard, and spared them from incineration. The cornetist later recalled:

"A whole crowd of people suddenly rushed toward us shouting and screaming. At least half of them jumped right overboard. It wasn't till a few seconds afterward that we saw the smoke and fire. The wind, luckily, was blowing the flames away from us. I got the family together [his wife and three children] and told them to stick close to me. I took my little August, three years old, on my arm and was considering the best place for safety when the deck broke and fell with the ruins. I still held my child, but my wife and the other children were torn away from me."

George Dillemuth, unlike Schneider, had no one with him. Saved from death by drowning, he stood on the shore, a dripping forlorn figure, and like a true musician mourned for his one and only *Schatz* ("treasure, sweetheart"): his beloved violin.

The last refuge aboard the burning boat was the main afterdeck. Here the members of Pastor Haas's party were in the women's cabin, surrounded by the crazed passengers forced back by the fire. "I found my wife near a sort of ladies' parlor at the extreme stern of the boat, which had been set aside for a few officers of the church and their families," the pastor reported. "There are two sliding doors to this parlor. I succeeded in closing one. The other I could not stir, so we were exposed to the flames which were sweeping through the ship — the woodwork in its path crackling and blazing fiercely."

Pastor Haas described the ghastly spectacle that followed:

"Women were shrieking and clasping their children in their arms. Some mothers had as many as three or four with them. ... The women and children clung to the railings and stanchions, but could not keep their hold. With my wife and daughter, I was swept along with the rest. I believe the first that fell to the water were crushed overboard. When they went, there seemed to be a general inclination to jump. The women and children went over the railings like flies. In the great crush many women fainted and fell to the deck to be trampled on. Little children were knocked down.

"I succeeded in getting two life preservers. ... One I tied about my wife, and the other I put on myself. I got my wife and daughter out on the rail. We remained close to the rail until the fire was close upon us. Then as I climbed over with my wife, somebody rushed between us — I was in such an excited state that I do not remember whether we were pushed or jumped."

When he struck the water, he sank, and when he came up again, he found scores of people about him fighting to keep afloat.

"One by one I saw them sink around me, but I was powerless to do anything. ... My preserver was of no avail, I cannot swim. I went down once, and when I came up, I clutched at the blade of the paddle wheel."

The pastor hung on for some time and was badly burned about the head and the beard. Eventually he was picked up by a tug. His wife and girl were gone.

The Reverend George Schultz of St. Luke's Church, Erie, Pennsylvania, a guest of the pastor, fared better.

"I was sitting forward of the stern talking with some teachers when the cry of fire came, and we saw the flame about the middle of the boat. The fire made a wall which cut the boat in two. ... I got a life preserver — pulled one down and held it by the strap. The weight of the life preserver broke the strap. I knew it was no good and threw it away."

61

There was then nothing to do but wait for outside help. Mr. Muller, a Sunday School teacher, and Schultz worked to quiet the children, who were shouting at one another to jump into the water. "We kept about fifty of them away from the rail . . . stood with our backs against it, hoping some boat would appear before the flames . . . drove us into the water. Finally a tug rounded the stern . . . and Mr. Muller and I dropped the children into it one by one until there were fifty on board. Then we jumped down and were taken to the island. The tug was the *Wade.*"

An eyewitness drawing of the Slocum *disaster.*

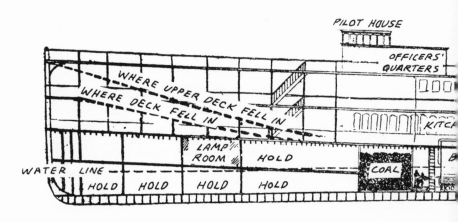

PILOT HOUSE

OFFICERS' QUARTERS

WHERE UPPER DECK FELL IN

WHERE DECK FELL IN

KITCH

LAMP ROOM

HOLD

COAL

WATER LINE

HOLD | HOLD | HOLD | HOLD

Terrified women and children, their bulky clothes aflame, stampede as the fire sweeps across the deck.

Diagram of the Slocum *showing where the decks collapsed.*

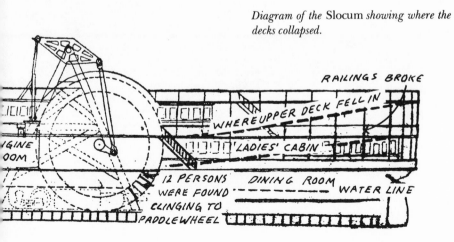

The raised hulk of the once palatial vessel after being submerged for eight days.

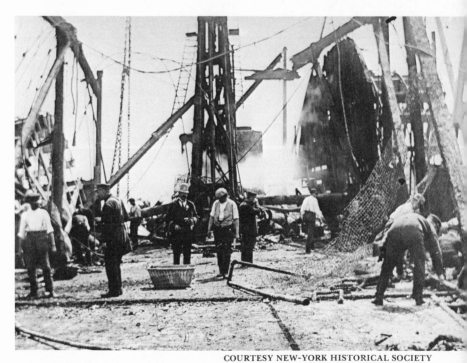

View of the main deck after the holocaust. The only wooden parts left were the water wheels. The chicken wire on the right was used to hold up the life preservers.

Policemen carrying corpses to one of the rescue boats.

Doctors and nurses on North Brother Island attend to the injured and lay out the bodies of the dead.

Half-crazed survivors on North Brother Island.

Relatives and friends of the Slocum's *passengers wait outside the morgue to identify their dead.*

(LEFT): *Mrs. Backman and her baby, whose bodies were found among the drowned victims on the beach.* (RIGHT): *Lizzie, Christina, Katie, and John Muth, who were aboard the* Slocum *with a party of eleven children, only two of whom survived.*

OPPOSITE PAGE: *Pier turned into a temporary morgue where dead bodies in coffins packed with ice await removal by friends and relatives.*

One of the many funeral processions to the Lutheran Cemetery in Queens.

THE FLOTILLA

FROM THE TOWER of the De La Vergne Refrigeration Building on the Bronx shore (now the R. Hoe Building), Herbert Nulson, the watchman, looked down to see the burning *Slocum* emerge from Hell Gate. After turning in an alarm to the police, he returned to watch the maneuverings.

At the sight and sound of the excursion boat, every craft in the bay turned toward her. The tug *Walter Tracey,* coming upstream directly behind, put on steam and gave chase. *New York Central Tug No. 17* cut loose a float it had in tow and followed. The tug *Wheeler,* heading straight for the *Slocum's* port side, made a quick maneuver, and the *Arnot,* coming downstream wide around Lawrence Point, turned to starboard, and both joined the train. The Health Department's ferry, *Franklin Edson* put out from her 132nd Street pier, and the tug *Goldenrod*, not five hundred yards directly offshore, turned;

they almost met as they fell into line, and the *Sumner, Margaret, Director,* and *Easy Times* joined the flotilla as well. Besides these, Nulson watched smaller craft put out from every point to converge on what was now a flaming nightmare, veering first toward the Bronx shore, then toward North Brother Island in the bay, trailing a wake of writhing, wailing humanity.

For the *Walter Tracey* it was a mad race after the burning boat. Captain Flannery called for full speed and ordered his men to lay the vessel alongside the *Slocum.* When contact was made, a rain of screaming children fell upon the tug's deck. The tugmen pitched into the rescue work so intently that few noticed that the soles of their shoes were sizzling from the burning deckboards underneath. It was not till the *Tracey's* pilothouse caught fire that Captain Flannery ordered the men to sheer off. The wails of dismay from the doomed vessel were too much for him, however, so he followed in the gruesome wake, with his men hanging over the sides reaching for each pitiful baggage that floated by. Those they missed disappeared.

When the *Slocum* ran up on North Brother Island, Flannery held back the tug for fear of grounding himself, but ordered away his lifeboats to pick up people in the shallow water. Then, with his deck crowded with shivering, frightened beings, the *Tracey* turned toward Port Morris on the Bronx shore to discharge the victims he had managed to save.

The men on the tug *Wheeler,* heading out of Port Morris bound for the Long Island shore, had the best view of the outbreak of the fire. Captain William N. Noble said, "I was coming down when I saw the *Slocum* coming up. I thought there was something queer about her at first, but I actually whistled twice at her — meaning I wished to cross her bow — before I saw a burst of flame from a forward hatchway. The whole steamboat was aflame in a minute."

Wheeler was towing a scow at the time, but Noble kept his head and did not order it dropped. "In an emergency," he said later, "a scow is a handy thing on which to climb." After stopping to let the *Slocum* pass, Captain Noble trailed behind her, picking up survivors.

Captain Van Elton, of the Keeler Transportation tug *Arnot*, recalled, "We were going toward New York when the *Slocum* hove in sight near Sunken Meadow. We ran within one hundred and fifty feet of her." Moving fast, Van Elton brought his boat alongside the starboard side of the *Slocum* — a position he was able to hold for a few seconds only. The swift steamer shot ahead of the *Arnot,* and the captain had to be satisfied to tag along until the *Slocum* was beached. Then, while the tug caught fire three times, Engineer Olsen and Fireman Anderson dived in and brought back six women and two children. After pulling his own dripping carcass aboard, Olsen then noticed three children floating near the shore and went in again. They were all tots under six, but Olsen could not manage the three at one time, so, holding two heads above water with his left arm, he swam to shore, then returned for the other. Greatly exhausted, Olsen then returned to the *Arnot* to lie down witht the fifteen other bodies on her deck.

Captain Hillery of the White Star Towing Company's *Goldenrod* also tried to overtake the *Slocum* but had to wait for the beaching before coming up to her. "I sighted her coming up in back of me about 132nd Street," he recalled. "I had the schooner *Allison* in tow. As she swept past me, I cast off the schooner and put on all speed after the *Slocum*. She went like the wind." Like the *Arnot, Goldenrod* only reached her after she had driven her nose on the sandbar at North Brother Island.

"Headfirst, sideways, anyways, hitting the rail, the deck, the water, men, women and children hailed down upon my decks from the *Slocum's* lower and middle decks," Hillery reported. "The crew and myself passed them to the stern, and then, with eighty-five maimed and crippled, either aboard or hanging from the bow, I put out for the Bronx shore. Back I ran, and with eighty-five more I raced for the New York shore. On the third trip the flames had eaten so far aft that I got only fifteen or twenty. I counted two hundred in all that I landed." (The numbers of people saved by the various rescue vessels were sometimes exaggerated.)

Unlike the *Goldenrod* and the *Arnot*, the *Franklin Edson*, a larger and more powerful steamer, was able to overhaul the *Slocum*. Starting from a dead stop at its 132nd Street pier, with Captain Henry Rock calling for full speed, it headed for the burning ship, and it was not long before the awful heat from the *Slocum* was blistering the fresh white paint on the immaculate Health Department ferry.

Some of the crew uncoiled a hose and kept playing a stream continuously on the *Edson*'s woodwork, while others took aboard fifty women and children and the lifeless bodies of ten more. Finally, the unbearable heat forced the captain to draw his boat away or lose the lives he now had on board. With the paint and gilt trimming melted, windows broken and scars from the fire streaking back thirty feet from her bow, the *Franklin Edson* turned away, unable to continue.

The tug *Director* nearby had another problem. She was in no danger of fire but her entire band of survivors rushed to the rear deck, which lifted her bow clear of the water, forcing the captain to maneuver the boat to shore at a most peculiar angle.

The crews of two boats, closest when the *Slocum* beached, watched from the island's pier as the roaring holocaust went by and ground up on the rocky shore: *the Massasoit,* a 153-foot steamer that served as a ferry for the Department of Correction, and the chunky tug *Wade.*

Both put out immediately and headed round the pier. Though closest behind the *Slocum* when she struck land, the *Massasoit,* because of her deep draft, had to stand fifty feet off; still, the waters teemed with struggling survivors, so there was plenty to do. Captain Parkinson cut loose his small boats, which were soon filled by gasping, desperate people scrambling for their lives.

In one boat alone, two deckhands pulled in eight people, while Mate Al Rappaport swam about bringing in a woman and seven children. As with other craft, a hose had to be played on the pilothouse and upper works to prevent fire, even at a distance, so intense was the heat.

The fireboat *Zophar Mills,* summoned by the first land-based fire company to reach the Bronx shore, picked up the firemen who had called for her, plus reserves from the Alexander Avenue Police Station, and made for the scene. By then the *Slocum* had beached herself. Policemen and fire laddies alike joined the rescue efforts. Fireman Plate of Engine Company 60 was nearly drowned himself, dragged down by the death grip of a drowning woman, and had to be pulled out by an assistant battalion chief.

The noise was such that it reached up to the New Haven Railroad's Mott Haven yards at 132nd and St. Ann's Avenue, where two tugs cut loose the flatboats they had in tow and made for the scene, picking up the yacht *Theo* on the way.

With each minute the *Slocum* burned, the number of rescue craft grew. From along the shores smaller boats were joining the fleet already under way. For every hundred spectators who watched helplessly, a few chose to do something, no matter what. They commandeered skiffs, dinghies, rowboats, any vessel in sight, and headed for the *Slocum*.

From their clubhouse in the dismantled ferry *Gerald Stuyvesant,* the members of the Stuyvesant Yacht Club put out to do their part. The motor-driven sloop *Easy Times,* from 140th Street, towed small boats into which people could climb. After rescuing about a dozen, she was almost capsized by frantic victims grabbing at the gunwales. Captain McGovern from the dredge off Astoria had already picked up five women and six children in his tiny launch *Mosquito,* all she could hold. From as far away as Steinway, Long Island, a bathhouse manager, spotting the *Slocum* cutting across the bay, cut short his breakfast and, after taking some policemen from the 74th Precinct aboard his launch *Gloria,* followed the wake of the doomed vessel and picked up twenty-two bodies.

Along the Bronx shore the boss of the shipway Marble Works at 135th Street knocked off work and sent his men out in any sort of craft they could lay their hands on. Reuben Tudor stopped cleaning his sloop *Surprise,* picked up his friend Granville Gibbons at the foot of Willow Street, and went out and saved several women. After picking up two drowned boys, who seemed to be held *under* water by their life belts, plus some rotten belts from the littered water, they turned away in disgust. Henry Berg, in his tiny overloaded rowboat nearby, did the same.

At 136th Street, Policemen Zuk and Holt of the Morrisania Station rowed out in a skiff to save six. Another policeman, James Collins, who had seen the *Slocum* first at 132nd Street, ran up to 138th Street, commandeered a yawl, and with Patrolman Hubert Farrell, sailor Olaf Jensen, and Sam Patchen, a Negro porter, went out to rescue twenty-six.

Sailors Scard and Wood, putting out from the same point, helped twenty women aboard other vessels, and two stevedores from the Sileck Lumber Yard jumped into a boat on the davits of a schooner, cut the falls, and set out for the *Slocum* before she beached. It was so hot under the lee of the fire they had to jump in the water to keep their clothes from burning off.

One of them said later, "I'll never forget the horrors we saw. There were so many women and children in the water we could hardly dip our oars without striking a head. We picked up the women and children by the hair. If they were alive, we drew them into the boat; if not, we let the dead drop back into the water to wait until we had rescued the living."

Though their faces and hands were blistered and sore, the two stevedores were happy. They had saved more than thirty.

At 141st Street a pair of policemen took over two rowboats. John Schwing got out to the paddle box and had his hair and beautiful handlebar mustache burned off while helping five people aboard. Bicycle Policeman Webster's heroics were less spectacular. He managed to pull in two boys, but in maneuvering a heavy woman into the flimsy boat, he capsized it and had to relinquish his wards to some other eager rescuer.

Help came from all sides, even the other side of the law. John Merther and Dan Casey, prisoners from the workhouse on Rikers Island, sighted the *Slocum,* jumped into a nearby boat and, judging all men equal in time of disaster, picked up Dr. Broder of the workhouse staff. They rowed to the burning boat and saved five people. Their short trip into the world of altruism was ended sooner than they expected, however, not by the police but by firemen. They collided with a fireboat.

Amid the din and confusion at the rescue scene, in an atmosphere charged with haste and excitment, two vessels remained apparently indifferent. The first was a sleek white craft flying the blue-and-white burgee of the New York Yacht Club. According to Robert D. Jackson, who watched from the Bronx shore, "Her captain deliberately withheld aid, which might have resulted in the saving of many lives. [The yacht] was about 110 or 115 feet long, with a white hull and yellow stack. He had the engines stopped and waited till the burning vessel was beached, then proceeded to a point off 140th Street on the city shore and came to. With field glasses he watched the destruction of the boat. The absolute callousness of the captain impressed me greatly."

Another and probably more accurate account was given by a Mr. Isaac Lurie: "The yacht lay in the channel between North Brother Island and Hunts Point [Bronx], that is the north

shore. Despite the screams, she steamed leisurely past the burning boat . . . around the northern part of North Brother Island.
The yacht [then] lowered a white dinghy from the starboard
side with two men in it."

Later, in a letter to the New York *Herald,* Mr. J. Bard of the
thus traduced yacht, *Candida,* refuted the no-assistance charges
and cleared the air considerably:

"We arrived from the eastward at the scene of the wreck as
the *Slocum* was beached, about 10:10. Our lifeboat was lowered
at once and sent to save life in charge of the mate, who had
begun picking up those persons hanging under the starboard
paddle box. The people were transferred to other boats."

The other vessel charged with failing to help was the
ferryboat *Bronx,* plying between 138th Street and College
Point, Queens. Captain Churchill of the sloop *Easy Times* said
the ferry passed and ignored the *Slocum.* Second Mate Corcoran of the *Slocum,* a master of exaggeration, said, "The ferry
Bronx refused to help. She was so near I got out the gangplank
ready to put out, but she kept on."

The fact is, the ferry had left the 138th Street slip at 10 A.M.,
as attested to by the crew and Patrolman Collins, who had
helped an old lady aboard and then walked six blocks
downtown, where he spotted the *Slocum* coming up the river.
The ferry, then, had been several minutes away from the shore
before the burning boat heaved into sight.

A passenger aboard the ferry later asked the captain why he
had rendered no assistance. The captain explained that in a
very narrow channel between rocks — and in *those* waters — any
attempt to turn around would have resulted in two wrecks
instead of one. The passenger looked back and wondered.

By now the roaring inferno that had once been a beautiful
ship was surrounded by a dozen tugs, two fireboats, a police
boat, steamers, yachts, launches, and a hundred other smaller
craft. Of all these men, none did more extraordinary

work than the tug *Wade,* named for its husky owner and engineer.

Jack Wade was as tough as the boat he owned. He had his captain, Robert Fitzgerald, drive the pugnacious tug so close to the burning *Slocum* that the hair on his arms frizzled, and the shirts of three of the crew were burned off their backs. As he told it: "I was lying at the dock at North Brother Island, getting water, when I saw the *Slocum* coming up the river [on fire, a fire portside forward]. . . . I cast loose and cast the hose off and made for the *Slocum* as quick as the Lord would let me."

Launching her lifeboat and throwing life belts to the people in the water, the *Wade,* which drew only four feet of water, went right on up the beach after the *Slocum*, cutting under her stern.

As the *Wade* approached, the *Slocum*'s afterdeck collapsed, pouring a torrent of people onto the tug's tiny deck, Mate Flanagan among them. The *Wade* then went along the *Slocum*'s starboard side, close to the shore, while its crew dived in and brought out survivors.

"I had seven men aboard," said John Wade, "and they didn't lose any time pulling people in. I told them never mind the dead, we'd attend to them afterward. Get the ones that were alive first."

One of the deckhands, Ruddy McCarrol, almost did himself in with his heroic efforts. After putting over half a dozen onto the *Wade*'s deck, Ruddy went back for just one more poor soul, who turned out to be a hefty German woman. Getting her over the rail singlehanded was almost too much, but McCarrol succeeded finally, and then flopped face down on the deck himself, exhausted.

Suddenly the woman revived, shook Ruddy, and yelled, "Vake up! Vake up! There is my liddle Klaus in the vater!" and shoved him back in. The weary deckhand managed to get

81

himself and the child aboard somehow — the *Wade*'s 155th rescue — and then fell in a faint.

"I want to say this," Wade reported later. "The two men in the wheelhouse — I suppose the captain and the pilot — and the man at the engines must have been the last to leave."

The men in the wheelhouse stuck till it was no use to stick any longer, Wade maintained. He then saw one cross himself (Van Wart) and jump overboard, followed by the other. He said to his men, "Boys, the engineer's a goner." He had seen the vessel backed clear up to the beach, so he knew someone must be in the engine room, but he did not expect him to get out.

"Yes, some of the *Slocum*'s men helped me after they got aboard," said the tugman, "but I put that fellow Flanagan ashore. He cast off a line [attaching the tug to the *Slocum*] — afraid, I guess, that my boat would catch fire and that he was risking his skin again. I went for him, and, well — oh, I just put him off the boat, that's all."

KAHNWEILER'S
NEVER SINK
LIFE PRESERVERS

THE TINY *WADE*, which had come up under the counter of the *Slocum*, its bow reaching toward the starboard paddle box, was bearing the brunt of the overflow from the decks above. Men, women, and children jumped or were thrown into the arms of the husky tugmen. Clattering down with the rest was the hulk of First Mate Ed Flanagan, later to spin a yarn of his selfless heroism.

According to Flanagan, he had been everywhere. He hurried to Conklin with the news of the fire, then to Captain Van Schaick, who ordered full speed to North Brother Island; he then appeared at the engine-room door again to tell Brandow to turn on the water, and on the upper deck he spent two hours trying to restore order. (From first to last, the disaster did not exceed twenty-two minutes.) He remained there till his clothes caught fire, then reappeared in the engine room with Brandow.

"The assistant engineer and I were the last to leave the hold of the boat," he would boast. "We jumped into ten feet of water. As I jumped, the afterdeck fell and carried down a lot of people. I swam over to North Brother Island and was so exhausted I could hardly walk. A nurse gave me a drink of whiskey and revived me." In addition to all this, Flanagan tried to rescue a woman and two children — he said.

In point of fact, Flanagan panicked. When the fire hose burst, he with the rest of the crew followed the tide of humanity to the afterdeck, shouldered his way to the rail, and waited for one of the rescue craft to come close. When the *Wade* appeared, he leaped aboard and even then did not recover from his fright, but tried to cast off the line holding the tug to the *Slocum* and was soundly berated for his cowardice by the tug's crew and doughty Jack Wade. It was perhaps at that time he made his leap "into ten feet of water," and since the assistant engineer was only then jumping from the *Slocum*, they may well have splashed down at the same moment.

Brandow had remained in the engine room and responded to every signal from the pilothouse from the first "full speed ahead" to the last "stop." He then made his way above decks to dive in just forward of the starboard paddle box.

Just abaft this, in a small room housing the donkey engine, Chief Engineer Ben Conklin had been performing an act of futile heroism: standing by the pump, which was delivering sixty pounds of water pressure to an open standpipe on the forward deck — from which the hose had long since been blown off. When Flanagan had come to him with news of the fire, he had told Brandow to stay with the engine and had run across the main deck to man the pump.

"The part of the boat where I stood was filled with a dense black smoke," he would say later. "I was obliged to cover my mouth with my arm in order to breathe. . . . The thunder of feet above my head was terrific as people made a rush for the

84

rear and sides of the boat. . . . A dense cloud of smoke rolled from the forward deck and completely covered the lower part of the vessel." Conklin, to escape suffocation, staggered out into the blinding cloud to be caught up in the stampede and swept onto one of the tugs alongside. Despite Jack Wade's foreboding, despite their own devotion to duty, both engineers survived.

Deckhand John Coakley, who had bungled everything else till now, also managed to come off with his life. He was quite candid about it:

"When the hose burst, I guess I lost my head. The flames were gathering headway, and in a minute it seemed the forward part of the boat was a mass of flames. Some of the people who saw the hose burst ran upstairs yelling, 'Fire!' and . . . I ran upstairs after them. . . . Then I pulled down the wires that held the life preservers in the racks . . . and they fell down on the deck row after row. Then I grabbed a baby and jumped overboard. . . . It took only three or four strokes to get on the beach after we grounded on the island bar, and I was able to walk ashore."

Another bungling deckhand, Dan O'Neill, made a more spectacular but disastrous escape. O'Neill — who had stored the dry hay in the tinderbox belowdecks the night before — added another mark to his record of misjudgments. He decided to join the occupants of an overcrowded rowboat despite their protests. He justified his behavior later by saying that he intended to take command of the boat below and "help them manage it." (O'Neill had served aboard the *Slocum* for a total of two months and in that time had not even been trained in lifeboat drill.) He jumped into the boat, capsized it, then swam for shore, helping no one.

On hearing the groan of the keel on the rocky bottom, the stokers had come abovedecks. One went over straightaway.

The other, Michael Lee, tried a few life belts first, then jumped overboard without one.

Most of the crew had gone over now except the two in the galley. Through the thin bulkhead Cook Canfield had heard the signals from the engine room just ahead:

"I heard two bells and a jingle, and I knew that meant there was something doing, for that means 'Backwater powerful hard.' I ran up and saw there was a fire and shouted, 'Boy, come up.' " Young Robinson, who was peeling potatoes, pocketed his knife, came on deck, got a life belt, and jumped in along with Canfield, who already had one. The two were immediately set upon by drowning passengers. In their frantic efforts to attach themselves to Canfield, fear-crazed women tore the shirt from his back and grabbed at his life belt. "I can swim," he said later. "so when a lot of people got hold of my preserver, I unfastened it and helped them into a boat that came along." He couldn't save them all, however. "One woman, a handsome one she was, said, 'If you save my life, you won't have to work for the remainder of your life.' I'd have liked to help her but I couldn't."

Canfield swam about helping those he could till he laid his hand on the stern of a nearby rowboat and someone growled, "Turn loose of that." The big black man had heard it all before; he understood. "I want to get these *women* in, that's all I want to do," he explained. At this the boatman took the women aboard but not Canfield. The embittered man swam to the *Massasoit* and pulled himself aboard.

Robinson, still in the water, had no such trouble; on hearing someone yell, "Save those boys," he had come between two lads locked in a fight for survival, separated them, and dragged them over to the starboard paddle wheel.

Under the paddle-wheel housing a score of shivering frightened people were clinging to the buckets, among them Pastor Haas, Mrs. Kassebaum, and Payne the porter, who had made it there, he said, by "paddling like a dog." In this cool, dank, dripping cavern, they waited for deliverance, listening to cries from mangled forms above and the pleas of the drowning outside.

Michael McGrann was one of those drowning.

A woman survivor later told that, alerted by a wild scramble of feet overhead and a little cloud of smoke that something was wrong, she turned to an excited man in a nearby stateroom to ask if there was any danger. "He was . . . hurriedly putting a lot of money in a small bag, [but] he assured us there was [no danger] at all. [Then] he took his money and hurried away. I have since learned that he was the purser."

Michael McGrann was actually a steward on the *General Slocum,* not the purser, and as Ed Flanagan said, he was trying to save the ship's money — "It was mostly silver; more than a thousand dollars was in the bag."

McGrann had emptied the ship's safe, donned a life belt brought to him by a waiter, and jumped overboard with his heavy burden. He was drowned — by the money he was trying to save, perhaps for the company that had allowed its life belts to deteriorate to uselessness.

Around McGrann others were being pulled under by these same life belts. "Kahnweiler's Never Sink Life Preservers," after thirteen years of neglect, had become malicious, inanimate weights, dragging down the victims they were supposed to buoy up.

Little Lucy Rosenagel, bewildered by it all, literally tried to preserve her life preserver. "In the water the life preserver burst or came apart. I had also grabbed a camp chair when I jumped overboard, and I held on to that and tried to keep the life preserver from falling apart by bunching it up with my arm. A lot of powder was running out of it. I kept up till a man in a rowboat grabbed me and pulled me into the boat."

Those, like Lucy, who had jetsam to cling to made the most of it. Some grabbed at straws, like Ernie Greenhagen's hat. "A woman grabbed at me just as I was going over," he said. "She got my hat. . . . I saw her throw the hat into the water and jump after it. She went down at once."

Little Frieda Gardner, whose life belt was torn off her body aboardship, made it with a piece of wood and a prayer. "A man picked me up and threw me in the water. I saw him a second later swimming toward me, and it gave me courage. But then, he disappeared. A plank came floating by, and I grabbed it. It easily supported me."

Somebody caught Frieda by the foot, then let go. She kept trying to pray, but a bad conscience got in the way — she had gone on the excursion without her mother's knowledge.

"A man grabbed the plank and was pulling himself on it" she said, "when a woman threw her arms about his neck, and the two slipped back into the water. I managed to say a prayer [and] then felt better. . . . I resolved never again to disobey my mother." Finally a man in a rowboat reached over and pulled her in.

Thus the debris surrounding the burning ship served to save more lives than the "life preservers" themselves. Every bit of flotsam at hand was used to keep someone alive — camp chairs, deck chairs, tables, anything. One boy of six floated to safety hugging his toy hobbyhorse.

Of all the objects floating near the *Slocum* that day, the largest and most buoyant mass was undoubtedly the portly form of Police Officer Albert T. Van Tassel of the River and Harbor Squad. Van Tassel, who had sailed on the *Slocum* to keep order and to ensure the safety of the excursionists, had been caught in the mad crowd on the main afterdeck. After the beaching, he climbed over the rail to help the children off. "I stood on the outside of the rail, passing the children into the tugs and trying to keep order. . . . Every time I saw a little face turning its pitiful appeal to me, I thought of my own two children at home."

Being in uniform, Van Tassel attracted the attention of many women, and scores of them rushed up and begged him to save them. "God knows, I wish I could have done so," he said later.

Van Tassell's peculiar position on the rim of the fantail not only saved the lives of many children, but his own as well. The main deck jutted out a few feet beyond the ones above. Therefore, Van Tassell missed being crushed to death when the upper decks fell. He did, however, receive a heavy blow on the back of the neck and fell unconscious into the water.

"I thought it was the deck that hit me," he said, "but the people who saw say it was the body of a big fat woman who jumped from the deck above."

When he struck the water, he found himself, of course, in the midst of many desperately drowning passengers, most of them women. "The women all grabbed for me, and for a time it seemed as if I would go down. The water . . . revived me, and I started for shore. I found that I was too weak to swim, so I turned over on my back to float. I was soon surrounded [again] by women and children, grabbing at me to save themselves. I called to them to keep calm, and I would save them. Then I floated to North Brother Island with women and children clinging to me from head to foot."

This living life raft was navigated toward the shore by its "passengers," where it was pulled from the water by J. J. Owens, a bricklayer. After everyone had disembarked, the stout officer stood upright and, with Owens, helped his fellow policeman, Kelk, ashore.

James J. Owens was one of those on the island when the great white vessel emerged from Hell Gate, its starboard side gleaming in the morning sun. Seen against the bright green fens of Sunken Meadow, he thought it formed a beautiful marine painting — an excursion boat bound for some sylvan grove.

For a moment the peaceful tableau held its pristine beauty.

Then, as if a mad artist had stabbed at it, an orange-red blot burst across the canvas. A wild hand drew the colors up and over the ship, streaking feathers of flame through the sky, and the sleek vessel was outlined by a halo of fire. As Owens watched, the flaming horror turned and headed straight toward him.

North Brother, like so many other river islands in New York, was used as a site for hospitals — particularly, considering its isolated location, as a center for contagious diseases. The burning *Slocum* beached herself within two hundred feet of the northern wing of Riverside Hospital, the principal facility, then crammed with measles and scarlet-fever victims.

Aghast at the holocaust that had landed almost on top of them, the staff converged at the water's edge — doctors, nurses, everyone who could walk. The bedridden followed.

"Patients in the contagious wards, especially the scarlet-fever ward," Dr. Darlington of the Board of Health reported later, "went mad with the thing they saw from their windows and went screaming and beating at the doors until it took fifty nurses to quiet them."

Nevertheless the staff ran to the northern shore and formed a rescue cordon along the waterfront from the pier to the retaining wall.

First to break ranks was Pauline Pultz, a teenage waitress. "As soon as I saw there was a big vessel on fire," she said, "I pulled off my Oxford ties and ripped off my apron. They tried to hold me back by my skirt, but I let them pull the skirt off me and rushed into the water in my petticoat."

Calling for the mothers to throw their babies overboard, she swam out and reached the starboard paddle box just as a baby was disappearing in the churning water beneath the paddle wheel's last turn. Pauline pulled the baby out, took her ashore, and, on seeing the little thing's jaw dislocated, she set it. She then went back in with a lifeline to rescue three young women.

Her heroics ended when she was caught in a death grip by a

large woman. The stranglehold about her neck was too much. "I had to fight for my life," she recalled later. "When they dragged us out, I fainted."

Other rescuers flocked to the shore. The fire-fighting force of the island formed a human chain to pass people back to the shore. Mary Maher, a helper in the measles ward, waded in and saved three boys and a woman. Margaret Lawrence, another helper, went in without stockings and rescued another ten. Dr. McCloughlin, in charge of the T.B. patients, took a rowboat and picked up six people. Mary McCann, a measles patient, rescued twenty. After pulling in the unsinkable Patrolman Van Tassel, James J. Owens, the bricklayer, joined his friend George W. Johnston, mate of the *Franklin Edson*, who was visiting him that day. Together they managed to pull eighteen to safety, although they had to row through a sea of dead bodies to get to the living. Drs. Lord, Weihman, Herowitz, Cannon, Algeson, and Watson leaped into boats and rescued many women and children, assisted by male orderlies and nurses, then went ashore to revive the people as they were brought in.

Mrs. White, superintendent of nurses, took on the task of resuscitating the victims. "As soon as a body was brought in," she said, "a nurse went to work to resuscitate it. Some nurses were asleep when the accident occurred. They threw their mackintoshes over their nightdresses . . . rushed down with bandages and medicants . . . worked over dripping bodies till they were wet to the skin. . . . At first we had no barrels; so we rolled them over our knees."

While the nurses labored to revive comatose victims, Mrs. White went back and got whiskey, more bandages and cheesecloth. Then she started out to see if she could do some rescuing herself. She tried several times to approach the burning wreck, but the heat was so intense that she was driven back. Finally, putting the skirt of her dress over her face, she was able to wade out up to her knees.

91

"The call came for ladders," she said. "There was no one to go for them, so I went. They were thirty-five feet long and dreadfully heavy, but I dragged them down to the water."

The ladders Mrs. White brought down were slid, like floating piers, out into the deeper water for victims to clamber onto. Long boards, too, served this purpose, and oars, boat hooks, garden rakes, and other extensions of the helping hand reached out to pull in the drowned and drowning. The number of helpers on shore grew till they equaled the multitude of rescuers in the water, who passed the dying into their hands.

Not everyone surrounding the ship was a Good Samaritan, however. Some had come to plunder and rob the dead. Bodies, some still in the water, were stripped of jewelry and other valuables which were passed along to other boats for "rescue." Emboldened by their success with the dead, some dared to rob the half-dead. Martha Weink recalled having rings, earrings, and brooch ripped off and then being pushed back into the water. August Lutjens, the teenage bartender, saw the nightmare with his own eyes:

"Dozens of small boats gathered around. In them I saw a lot of tough-looking men who, instead of assisting those in the water, shoved them away with a long pole and struck the hand that now and then grabbed hold of the side of the boats. . . . I heard one of these men shout, 'Give me two dollars, and I will save you.' Another offered to take me into the boat for all the money I had and my watch. Not only did the men demand pay for saving lives, but they actually robbed the people struggling in the water. I saw men . . . tear gold chains and watches from women and girls and . . . one man tear an ear from a fifteen-year-old girl in order to steal an earring."

Meanwhile the wreckage continued to burn — a giant holocaust raging sky high. And yet, in the dark gaping windows of the women's cabin aft, forms of the living could still be seen.

It seemed impossible that anyone could still be alive aboard the vessel, but suddenly a little boy, no more than six, was seen running along the top deck to the flagstaff at the bow. With difficulty he mounted the railing, grabbed the flagstaff, and started shinnying up away from the fire. The crowd ashore cheered him on, and with each jump of the flames he climbed higher and higher until he was almost at the top. Then the flagstaff began to tremble and fell back into the flames, carrying the child with it.

By now, the rooms, cabins, saloons were gone. The polished walls, fluted pilasters, sculptured columns had turned to ash, the red velvet to cinders. The shock of grinding to a halt had weakened supports, shattered mirrors and windows. Now the skeleton, eaten away by the cancerous heat, was crumbling. Column fell upon column, beam upon beam, deck upon deck. Fore and aft the vessel's superstructure collapsed.

THE AFTERMATH

At 10:20 a.m. it was all over. In less than thirty minutes after the little boy had discovered the fire, in less than fifteen after it had exploded into open flames, the ship was almost completely consumed. Of the metal parts, the only things remaining were the walking beam, the giant piston, the boilers, and the tall, blackened funnels. Of the wooden parts, there were still the hull, the thick timbered gallows frame, the hogback frames, and the paddle boxes. The port paddle-box roof was gone, its sides charred, but the starboard, by one of those vagaries of fate, was untouched. The gleaming white paint was unblistered, the intricate carvings — the flowery arcs, the ornaments along the outer rim, the design in the lunette and the gold and black letters: "GEN'L SLOCUM" — were perfectly preserved.

To prevent the fire from spreading to the hospital and other buildings on the island, the burning ship was pulled off the beach and out into the main stream, where the tide bore the smoldering sepulcher to its resting place. At a spot about seven hundred feet off Hunts Point, the *General Slocum* went down by the stern in ten fathoms. On hitting the bottom, she rolled onto her side, coming to rest at an angle of forty-five degrees. Her starboard paddle-box face remained well above water, marking her grave like the shield of a fallen warrior.

Along the shores, the ill-fated ship had left a grisly wake: hundreds of bodies, each identifiable by signs familiar to loved ones. Papa, with his tobacco-stained teeth, now a bloated gargoyle in a blue serge suit. Sister in her new sacque frock and her Oxford ties. Brother in his knickers and patent leather shoes. And Mama, too, in her white shirtwaist, full black skirt, and three petticoats — all the burdens of vanity that had pulled her under — her Gainsborough turban still fast on her head, the pink muslin roses singed. Lovers were found in a last fearful embrace, babies clinging to mothers, children strewn in violent postures of agony, bodies in blackened finery, faces twisted in a rictus of terror.

Some bodies had sunk beneath a pall of black water, the silt of the river drifting over their lifeless forms. Others were moved by the currents to other places — some to emerge on the shore of the Bronx, some on the island, minutes, hours, days apart. On the first day 498 bodies were recovered. By the next day the number rose to 561. It was estimated that 545 were still missing, and that, in all, probably 900 were dead — an estimate that would later be changed to 1,021.

The grim business of recovering bodies went on long into the night of June 15 and would continue for days after. Toward the end of the search, after a thunderstorm had brought up many bodies, the idea of using explosives suggested itself, and so, dynamite and cannon were brought into play to hasten the recovery of the *Slocum*'s dead. Under the supervision of Police Inspector Albertson, sticks of dynamite were attached to short pieces of timber, the free ends riding clear of the water while the dynamite sank to several feet below. These improvised mines were placed at intervals of one hundred yards around the wreck and set off by time fuses. Then, two artillery fieldpieces were put aboard a float to be towed around the wreck and back to the island. Firing began as soon as the tug and float had cleared the shore and continued till the hull of the *Slocum* was reached and thirty rounds had been fired. The floating battery then circled Rikers Island, discharging guns at short intervals until it was abreast of the pier on North Brother Island, where six rounds were fired. Within five minutes after the last volley, sixteen bodies rose. Further search in the wake of the battery revealed fourteen more.

If the work above the water was grim, in the bizarre world below, it was gruesome. Diver Charles P. Everett, who had explored the sunken battleship *Maine* for the United States government in 1898, was recruited to examine the ruins of the *General Slocum* on the day of the disaster. His report was an eloquent description of the underwater scene:

"With assistants and the crew of the steamer *William E. Chapman* I started for the scene of the disaster. . . . I was inside the 175-pound diving suit by 6:15 P.M. The *Slocum*'s . . . low side was in twenty-five feet of water, her stern in about sixty.

"Although the parts above water sweltered from the slowly dying heat, there was little smoke to impede my work. I was commissioned, if possible, to loosen the debris and beams [to free] any bodies in the hold and to make a general survey. . . .

"If I had not known what caused the frightful wreck I would have thought an explosion of some character had ripped the very bowels from the vessel and torn and lacerated her superstructure. The wreck was complete, absolute. . . . The appetite of the fire must have been insatiable. . . . Finally, after surveying the surface, I went slowly down into the tomb.

"While groping about in an endeavor to remove an intricate

mass of wire rail guards from my path . . . I noticed a section of the hold, on my right, sag less than a foot. Immediately the ends of dresses, and long, slowly moving, disheveled hair floated about from under the beams and general wreckage.

"I was at this time about the middle of the vessel. I crawled gingerly through the gloomy, disemboweled section to amidships. I thought I had my nerves under control. But I had only a foretaste of the real extent of this calamity. . . .

"There were at least eighty charred and pitiful distorted bodies of women and children in the center of the vessel. . . . I finally came to the conclusion, after making many efforts to extricate the bodies, that nothing but machinery can raise the shapeless mass of metal and wood that lies between the poor victims and human burial.

"The shadow of the walking beam — one of the [few] objects protruding above the surface — fell athwart something which was held, as in a vise, by a stanchion of what used to be a taffrail. A beam lay on it, and on the beam lay the pitiful little frame of a child whose dress was held in the clutches of the thing beneath — the mother evidently. I braced myself for what was to come and I peered around.

"Over on the leeward, or port side, where the debris lay in a shapeless heap . . . there were more things. Oh, a score of them! All caught in that implacable, fatal grip supplied by the crunching together of beams . . . stanchions . . . wooden supports and a thousand and one appurtenances of every excursion steamer.

"One by one, so far as I could avoid the obstacles and prevent my [air] lines becoming tangled in the maze, I tried to extricate the forms of those for whom mothers, or brothers, or sisters were wailing in hospitals or homes. A couple of bodies floated free of the tanglewood, but drifted away slowly — like the movement of a funeral, I thought at the time — into the dark, obscure corners of the thing that men used to call a graceful, speedy steamer. . . .

97

"A small group impressed itself indelibly upon my memory. Three children and a woman, who certainly was their mother, were pinioned against what I took to be part of a cabin detached from the whole. The children clung to her dress as if the life was still throbbing in their little hearts. But the mother, with a look of agony on her face, was kept from grasping the little ones by a big piece of iron . . . which lay diagonally across her breast. . . .

"They tell me I was down in the tomb about an hour and a half. That must be a mistake. I was down there a year."

Many of the bodies were never seen again, swept away by the tide. Others came to light far from the wreck. Seven-year-old Margaret Heim was found floating near the foot of Clinton Street in lower Manhattan, eight miles down the East River. When it was brought in by a tug, a woman in the crowd on the pier remarked, "It's Maggie Heim — her home is just up one block and around the corner."

Others were brought home by a less direct route. The corpses collected on North Brother Island and at the foot of 138th Street on the Bronx shore were transferred by boat to the city morgue or by wagon to the 35th Precinct police station at Alexander Avenue. Among these was the body of eleven-year-old Clara Hartman. Anonymously tagged "Number 24," she was laid on the station-house floor awaiting identification, but little Clara was not about to join the list of dead. She remembered:

"I was lying on something hard and . . . my head was covered. Then there was talking about taking the dead people away, and then I remembered the fire and the people drowning all around me. I thought I was still in the water. . . . My stomach got sick. I had swallowed a whole lot of salty water, and I did want awfully to get rid of it. Then it began to gush out of my mouth, and a woman said, 'This little girl ain't dead,' and she called, 'Doctor, doctor,' quick like that."

They pulled the cover off the child's head, and as she found herself breathing good air, she began to feel better. "Then they took me up from the floor and put me on a soft couch . . . I was taken to the hospital, where they treated me nicely."

Clara had returned to life in a place beseiged by hundreds of people, in search of loved ones — most from the St. Mark's neighborhood, clamoring, fighting, breaking through police lines to find the missing child they *knew* was inside.

Among those at the station house was a gaunt, wet, shivering figure: Captain William Van Schaick. The dazed man, urged on by eager reporters, was rambling on and on, half truth, half fantasy:

"We started from the East Third Street dock on schedule time, about nine thirty o'clock. . . . We were off Sunken Meadow when a fireman came up to me in the pilothouse and said there was a fire forward on the port side of the ship. We have had fires on the *General Slocum* before, but we have always been able to handle them. I had no idea that the fire would get away with us.

"The first thing I did was to call upon the men to take the steps necessary. There were twenty-three of them. . . . They set to work, but as I looked back, I already saw a fierce blaze . . . the wildest I have ever seen. I started to head for 134th Street, but was warned off by the captain of the tug who shouted . . . that the boat would set fire to the lumber yard and oil tanks there. Besides I knew the boat would founder if I put her there. Then I fixed on North Brother Island. . . .

"The crew did herculean work with the fire apparatus . . . under Mate Ed Flanagan and had two streams of water at work. They did noble work, but it was no use. The boat was as dry as tinder and burned like a match. . . ."

In a last plea for absolution the captain blurted out, "It was a good boat. I went over her myself last night, and everything was all right. God knows what caused the fire. It may have started

99

... in the kitchen." Then he broke down and begged, "Take me to the hospital, I'm a sick man." With this he and pilots Van Wart and Weaver were taken to Lebanon Hospital — under arrest.

Little Willie Oettinger had been passed from boat to boat and person to person till he, too, ended up in a hospital. There, though badly burned, the spunky thirteen-year-old resented being detained. Sixty-eight years later he recalled how he, his mother, three brothers, and a sister had joined the church excursion on the *General Slocum*. After the vessel had been beached, he tried to get into a tug, but it was too full. He looked for his family, but could not find them in the confusion.

"I was one of the last ones on the boat when I jumped off," he remembered. "I burned the top of my head, my hands, my leg ... my ears. . . . I jumped in the water and there was a hole in ... the *Slocum*. . . . I held on to that hole till two men in a rowboat motioned to me: 'Come on, come on, we'll take care of you, come on, start swimming.' They couldn't get near the boat, they said, 'It's too hot.' "

Willie started swimming toward the rowboat, where he was hauled aboard. From there they transferred him to a coal barge and from the barge to a tugboat and from the tugboat to the pier at 138th Street in the Bronx.

"From there I went to Harlem Hospital. Well ... in the hospital I had seen my clothes, which were wet, of course, hangin' on the line out in the back. So I got a little restless, and I said, 'I can't stay here, ain't nothin' the matter with me. I . . . got outa bed, went outside, took the clothes, brought 'em in . . . put 'em on and left. . . . "

He went to the nearest transit line — he thinks it was the Second Avenue El — and told the man that he didn't have the money for his fare. "The man at the station says, 'You were on that *Slocum*?' I says, 'Yes.' He says, 'You don't need any fare, go ahead on the train.'

100

"Well, when I got off the train, all the kids in the neighborhood seen me, and I asked them if they had heard anything about my mother . . . brothers and sisters . . . none of them knew. I went up into the house, and the first ones I seen was my sisters." Willie had three older sisters, who worked and hadn't gone on the excursion. "They told me that they had seen my name in the paper but they hadn't heard anything about the [others]."

News had drifted into the neighborhood bit by bit with each survivor who appeared. Twelve-year-old Freddie Mazeroth, one of the first to arrive, walked past St. Mark's and was surrounded by neighbors pleading for news of the disaster. Almost in tears, he ran home. Later, Nicholas Balzer, who had taken Peter Fickbaum's children on the excursion, staggered into Fickbaum's saloon at the corner of Seventh Street and Avenue D to tell his story. Then little Willie Oettinger came home to tell his. All, of course, were too stunned by what they had seen to wonder how the news could have preceded them.

It had been spread by the New York *Evening World*, which had received a telephone tip from an anonymous eyewitness to the horror. Galvanized into action, the city editor dispatched a dozen or so reporters to the scene of the disaster and detached another man to visit St. Mark's in search of a list of excursionists. The newspaper scored a famous scoop, and the word leaked out in Little Germany: The Seventeenth Annual Excursion had met with catastrophe.

At first a crowd gathered in front of St. Mark's Church, expecting words through some divine channel; the more realistic went to the house of Pastor Haas on Seventh Street. Here the minister's nineteen-year-old son, the only one of the family who had not joined the excursion, was learning over the telephone that his parents, two aunts, and a sister had perished on the

101

Slocum. It would be hours before he would hear that his father, at least, was safe.

Shortly after noon the crush of anxious relatives became so great around the pastor's house that it was decided to establish a temporary bureau of information in the church. Long tables were set up in the vestibule, and a sign was posted outside asking survivors to report their safety and advising relatives to inquire about those missing. Within a few minutes the street between First and Second avenues was packed. Policemen of the 14th Precinct were busy all day and night, maintaining order in the line of those who sought to enter. As the news came from the scene of disaster and newspaper offices, it was posted outside. At first only lists of the dead were posted. Later lists of the survivors went up. In this way many on line learned of the fate of their relatives. All that Wednesday night a quiet, grief-stricken crowd stood in front of St. Mark's Church. Dawn found them, silent with grief and fatigue, sitting or lying on the sidewalks, still patiently waiting for news.

For those with stronger stomachs there was another way to learn the dreadful truth: go to the morgue.

The facilities at the city morgue being quite inadequate for such a disaster, a temporary annex was improvised on the Department of Public Charities pier — a roofed-over edifice at the foot of Twenty-sixth Street. First Deputy Commissioner James Dougherty of the DPC later reported:

"At 10:30 news of the disaster reached the Department of Public Charities. We cut loose all our ferry service and sent out boats *Fidelity, Wickham, Companion,* and *Gilroy* to North Brother Island — and conveyed to the scene doctors and nurses from the City Hospital, Metropolitan Hospital, the Alms House and the Infants Hospital on Randall's Island and the Catholic chaplain, Father Broderick, from the latter place. . . . I ordered from Stolts, the wholesale undertaker on the Bowery, 200 coffins to be sent to North Brother Island and an additional 50 for the foot of Twenty-sixth Street." With these extras and the

DPC's own supply, Dougherty was able to coffin all that came down to him the first day. Tons of ice were also procured to preserve the bodies, and the grisly work of tagging, delivering, and identifying bodies began.

Of the 887 corpses brought from the island, over 600 were delivered by the Charity Department's ferry *Fidelity*, the rest by the Correction Department's *Massasoit*. As each boat arrived, the lifeless forms were tagged by Superintendent Fane of the morgue and placed in those crude polygons of wood that pass as coffins for the poor. Soon the long rows of caskets ran the length of the pier, and friends and relatives were wading through the ice water that was dripping from the dead, hoping they would never see a face, a dress, a remnant of cloth they knew. But their friends were there: The little boy in gray double-breasted jacket with large white pearl buttons? Four-year-old Harold Kircher. The red flannel sacque with large brass buttons? Amelia Klein, 13. The black satin-trimmed skirt, white blouse with lace front? Rosie Reiss, 30.

As each was identified and claimed, another voice swelled the chorus of lament. As each was carried out, the weeping blended, then was lost, in the clamor of the business world outside, where undertakers were fighting fiercely for the "privilege" of serving the bereaved.

Consolation was forgotten. In the heat of competition, voices were raised, fists flew, and even the dead were jostled as caskets were shunted from one wagon to another until they found peace in the hearse of the "winner." The police, busy enough holding back an army of frenzied friends, relatives, and morbid onlookers, were now faced with a battle within their own lines. Captain Shire of the 21st Precinct called in a few more reserves, nightsticks were raised, undertakers separated, and the procession of hearses, each bearing three and four caskets, moved out, peacefully conveying each body to its home — for the "funeral parlor" of the day was the front living room.

For days the hearses and wagons rumbled through the streets of Little Germany, delivering a tiny coffin here, several larger ones there. Crapes blossomed on every doorway, announcing the deaths within.

For Peter Fickbohm, a wife and three children. For Mr. Baumler, a wife and three. For Andrew Steil, a widower, four, his entire family. Mr. Steil, unlike some others, would be unable to bear up under it all. He would soon join his family by the only way he knew: suicide.

In a few days the funerals began. On June 18, the largest number were buried, 156 known dead, 29 unknown. The procession formed itself into a procession of twos — glass-enclosed hearses framed in finely carved ebony, drawn by dark horses draped in nettings of black — and moved out in the direction of the Williamsburg Bridge. Street by street new hearses and carriages of mourners fell into line and eventually were joined by fourteen vans from the morgue, carrying the charred remains of the unknown. The procession reached the entrance to the Williamsburg Bridge and spread across it like a pall, inching its way to Brooklyn.

On the Brooklyn side a few funerals dropped out to make their way to smaller cemeteries, but most kept on along Grand Street and onto Metropolitan Avenue, heading for the Lutheran Cemetery in Middle Village, Queens. Hundreds of sympathizers lined the streets along those long four miles. As the grim procession turned right into the cemetery gates, each hearse went its own way, clattering over cobblestoned drives to a private family plot, while the fourteen vans stopped at the site of a common grave. The 29 unknowns were buried there that day, to be joined later by 32 more. The following year a memorial would be erected to these 61 unknowns on the cemetery road renamed Slocum Avenue.*

*Each year on the Sunday nearest to the anniversary date of the disaster, services are held at this spot by the Slocum Memorial Committee of the Queens Historical Society.

104

The coroner's jury at the inquest into the Slocum *disaster. Inspector Lundberg is on the witness stand.*

(LEFT): *O'Gorman, coroner.* (RIGHT): *William Van Schaick, captain of the* Slocum.

John Coakley, deckhand, who discovered the fire aboard the Slocum, *and who lost precious minutes in reporting it.*

Josephine Hall, bookkeeper for the company that owned the Slocum.

(LEFT): *Henry Lundberg, assistant inspector of steamboats.* (RIGHT): *One of the life preservers that passed Lundberg's inspection.*

Memorial to over a thousand men, women, and children who died as a result of the General Slocum fire.

THE INQUEST

On MONDAY, JUNE 20, while funerals still rumbled through the streets and church bells tolled, a coroner's inquest opened. Since the coroner's office in Bronx Borough Hall at Tremont and Third avenues was deemed entirely inadequate to accommodate the huge crowd expected, the hearing was set up in the barnlike drill room of the Second Battery Armory, just a block away on Bathgate Avenue.

For the fifteen jurymen picked by Bronx Coroner Joseph Berry, a row of chairs fenced in by a rail of raw two-by-threes and -fours formed a crude jury box, placed to the right of the platform supporting the bench. The "bench," where Berry was to preside, was actually a long table with a high-backed upholstered chair behind it. To the right of the bench was the witness chair, upholstered too. For the relief and comfort of the jury, court staff, witnesses, and others, cuspidors were placed at suitable intervals, and at the corner of the bench platform, within easy reach, were two bottles of whiskey.

A number of exhibits were also to be seen, including one of the standpipes of the *Slocum*, sections of fire hose, life preservers, and other odds and ends retrieved from the sunken vessel.

As the meeting was about to start, the room was cleared of all except the witnesses and passengers injured in the disaster. Assistant District Attorney Francis P. Garvan called as his first witness Frank A. Barnaby, president of the Knickerbocker Steamboat Company.

Mr. Barnaby, who had dispatched a company investigatory team to the scene the day of the disaster, had issued a statement at four o'clock that same day, which painted a picture of a tight, well-ordered ship with a sharp, well-disciplined crew:

"We do not feel that our employees were responsible for the disaster since their discipline was perfect, and one minute after the fire started every man was at his post. We have frequent fire and boat drills aboard, and each man acted as he had been instructed. There were two policemen aboard who also, I understand, stood by. I believe that Captain Van Schaick did all in his power to save his passengers and I will back him in whatever course he pursues.

"The *Slocum* was fully supplied with all lifesaving devices, and I cannot understand why the passengers did not avail themselves of them. At the vessel's recent inspection we were told that she could safely remove all the passengers she was licensed to carry."

The day after the disaster, under questioning by the press, Mr. Barnaby had elaborated further on the safety of the *Slocum*. As for the fire-fighting equipment: "It was the best money could buy. The boat had been thoroughly overhauled this year at a cost of over $30,000 for refitting machinery, hose, extin-

guishing pumps, and other apparatus including life preservers
. . . the hose was all new. I am positive of it. . . . The inspectors
would not have issued a certificate . . . they are very rigid and
were not allowed any leeway."

As for the life preservers: "There were over 500 more than
required by law. . . . We put in 1,000 or 1,500 new ones this
year. . . . The *Slocum* was rated as an A-1 risk."

Wire to hold down the lifeboats? "No wires were used at all."
Why couldn't they be launched?" "People were killed in an
effort to get to them. A hundred failed in doing what one man
could have done." The life preservers were old and fell apart?
"When two people get hold of a single preserver, in their
frenzied effort to secure possession of it, they tear it apart. A
new preserver could be torn as easily as an old one. . . . They
were new before they were burned." The life preservers were
held up too tightly by the wires? "A little child could rip down
an entire length of wire with little exertion, which would drop
every preserver resting on it."

As the inquest progressed, these contentions of Mr. Barnaby
would, like the *Slocum* itself, quickly crumble.

At the request of the district attorney, Mr. Barnaby produced
a number of bills, which he claimed were for life preservers, fire
apparatus, and engines for the last three years.

"You know of your own knowledge that these bills are for
Slocum apparatus?" Mr. Garvan asked as he put them up for
evidence.

"I do," replied Mr. Barnaby.

Mr. Garvan then showed five bills dated from May 1902 to
May 1904. "You are sure all these were for the *General Slocum?*"

Mr. Barnaby was sure.

"If this is the case, how is it I find in some of these bills the
name *Grand Republic* scratched out or taken out with acid and
the name *Slocum* inserted?"

111

Mr. Barnaby did not know. "I suppose some bookkeeper must have done that," he said.

"What is the name of that bookkeeper?" asked Mr. Garvan. Mr. Barnaby did not know. He said that separate accounts were kept for the *Grand Republic* and the *General Slocum,* and that the books would show how many life preservers went to each. The books, it seemed, were kept in storage in Brooklyn, except those for the last three years. Mr. Barnaby believed they were there, but then, he did not think they kept the books after the business season ended. Annoyed by Barnaby's meanderings, Garvan asked, "Is it customary for a large firm to destroy its books?"

"I don't know," Barnaby mumbled.

Mr. Atkinson, secretary and general manager of the company, knew a little more. He said the bookkeeper's name was Miss Hall. She was the *only* bookkeeper they had, and he knew nothing about erasures on the bills. To clear up this point, Miss Hall was asked to appear, but did not — that day.

Next was to be Captain Van Schaick. He was on his way from the hospital, someone said, so John J. Coakley was called instead.

Coakley walked to the witness stand, removed his jacket and folded it across his lap, then sat slowly turning his derby in his hands.

Mr. Terence McManus, attorney for the Knickerbocker Steamboat Company, started off with an attempt to explode the myth about an ill-disciplined crew of drifters, but he misjudged his target. He asked Coakley if he had been drinking since the disaster; Coakley frankly admitted he had. McManus changed his tactics.

Q. — Were you ever present at a fire drill on the *Slocum?*
A. — I never was.
Q. — Were you instructed as to what to do in case of fire?
A. — Never.

Q. — How long have you been on the *Slocum*?
A. — Eighteen days.

Coakley then went on to tell the exasperated attorney of his unique method of counting passengers, described the mess in the forward cabin, and said the boy told him of the fire one minute after passing the Blackwell's Island lighthouse.

Q. — Did you ever light matches when you went down there
. . . in the forward cabin?
A. — Why, sure I did if I wanted to see.
Q. — Did the rest of the crew do the same?
A. — Sure they did.

Still hoping to save the company image, McManus asked finally if drinking beer was one of Coakley's duties. The deckhand said no and laughed.

If Coakley was of little help, Flanagan and his motley crew were of less. "Second Mate" Corcoran said he had never seen a fire drill aboard, though he had been with the *Slocum* for three seasons. He couldn't remember if any water came through the fire-hose nozzle. "First Mate" Flanagan waffled with each question asked.

At first, he did not remember if there were any new life preservers aboard the boat. Then he said, "They were all good. I guess some of them might have been bad." He conceded that he saw no life preservers except those marked "1891." Then he couldn't remember that he had taken down some twenty "new" preservers and told the inspector they were all like that. He said he did *not* go around the boat with the inspector. Then he admitted he ordered his men to take down "twenty, maybe ten." The rest, in the racks, were just poked at with a stick. Flanagan was firm on only one point. Asked for the second time whether any lifeboats were launched, he gave an unequivocal no.

On the second day of the hearing, Deckhand O'Neill told of capsizing the overcrowed rowboat he thought he could "manage." Assistant Engineer Brandow revealed that no steam could be turned into the forward cabin or any other part of the hold, although U. S. Steamboat Inspection Regulations provided that steam outlets should have been there. Then Miss S. C. Hall, bookkeeper for the Knickerbocker Steamboat Company, cleared up the mystery of the missing life belts.

Miss Hall admitted that she had erased the name *Grand Republic* from the bills and written in *General Slocum,* but only because she had heard Captain Pease say that the *Slocum* needed life belts and assumed that they were billed to the other ship by mistake. The next witness, Miss Reba Goldberg, bookkeeper for David Kahnweiler & Sons, denied that the preservers had gone to the *Slocum.* She testified that she had received an order for life belts for the *Grand Republic* from Captain Pease and had sent them to that ship. She did not remember selling any life belts for the *Slocum.*

The first witness of the afternoon session was Edward Weaver, second pilot of the *Slocum. The New York Times* noted that "Weaver answered all questions promptly and his demeanor was in marked contrast to the rest of the crew so far examined."

Weaver said that during the winter, life preservers were stored on board, and a lot of them, in the cabins, were allowed to remain in the racks all year. He recalled nothing of their inspection nor had he seen any used the day of the disaster, since there were none on the forward hurricane deck where he was stationed. The fire hose was not new but old and of the cheapest kind. Weaver told of buying some at the captain's orders. It was sixteen cents a foot (as compared to a dollar a foot for quality hose), two-thread linen and not rubber lined. He might have added that it had rotted in coils for years.

Assistant District Attorney Garvan now switched his ques-

tioning to determine the exact location of the ship at the time
Flanagan yelled up the blower — a point that would be argued
over for years by those who insisted the captain "knew" the
vessel was afire and should have landed in Hell Gate.

Q. — Now, how long was it between the time you got the
alarm of the fire until you went on the beach?
A. — Between two and a half and three minutes.
Q. — How far is it from Sunken Meadow to North Brother
Island?
A. — Between a half and five eighths of a mile.
Q. — Now, if you were in charge of the boat on that day,
where would you have beached her?
A. — In exactly the same spot.

Still convinced, as were many others, that the captain could
have landed elsewhere, the district attorney, referring to the
Bronx shore, asked Weaver: "If that boat had been put in at
Locust Avenue and 129th Street, wouldn't the wind have held
her the same as if she were anchored?"

A. — Certainly, but you couldn't put her in there. It would
have taken three minutes to swing her around in that tide, and
with that wind there wouldn't have been a soul alive to tell the
tale by the time we got there. The wind, which was blowing
across her quarter, would have swept all over the boat, and
everyone would have been roasted to death before landing.

The fateful maneuver that swept so many through the rails
on the afterdecks, when the *Slocum* swerved first towards, then
away from the Bronx shore, had cost another precious moment, one Weaver had not included in his reckoning. Flanagan's voice had come up the blower at 10:06 A.M.; the *Slocum*
had been beached at 10:10.

The next and last witness of the day was Henry Lundberg,
assistant inspector of steamboats. Mr. Lundberg was to be the

sensation of the day, if not the entire inquest. He was to stun the courtroom by taking a strong silent stand.

Four days before, in the fastness of his office at the Steamboat Inspection Service in the Whitehall Building, he had been quite glib. Under questioning by reporters he said:

"I went aboard the *Slocum* on May fifth and made a thorough examination as required by law. . . . I counted the life preservers and found that there were at least 3007, all in good condition. I did not reject one, knowing that the boat was licensed to carry 2,500 passengers. I asked Captain Van Schaick why there were more life preservers than required, one for each passenger and member of the crew. He told me that 500 new ones had recently been purchased, which accounts for the excess. Now I reiterate that all the life preservers I saw were in good shape and fit for use and each stenciled with the name *General Slocum* as required by law. If there were any more on board which were not good, I did not see them. It was not my business to know [that, as long as] they showed me the number that the law required."

"Did you try the straps on the preservers . . . ?" a reporter asked.

"Yes, I did, when I saw one that appeared in any way old, but I must say they were in good condition. I did not reject one. They were, as the law requires, placed easy of access overhead, resting on slats nailed to the carlings. They were in easy reach of any man who could with ordinary strength rip down a slat and a lot of life preservers would tumble down."

"Some of the preservers were held up by wire. . . ."

"The wire was so fine it could easily be torn down by almost anybody."

"You did not test the life preservers for buoyancy?"

"No, we never do that. That is done at the factory where they are made."

At the inquest Mr. Lundberg was not so glib. He said he had

been appointed from the civil service list in January, was still on probation until July. He was an inspector of hulls, his chief was James Dumont, his salary was $2,000 a year, and he inspected the *Slocum* on May 5 last; then his lawyer caught his eyes, and there were no more answers. Mr. Lundberg refused to answer on the grounds that it would tend to incriminate him.

The cornoner's jury was shocked, Assistant District Attorney Garvan stunned. "This is one of the most remarkable spectacles I have ever witnessed," he said, "an officer of the U. S. Government taking any such action."

Incensed at Lundberg's behavior, Garvan kept probing till he touched the sensitive spot.

Q. — Did you take any money from the *Slocum* people for your inspection?
A. — No, I don't do that sort of thing.
Q. — Did you make an honest inspection?
A. — Yes.
Q. — Then what can incriminate you?

Lundberg did not answer.

On the third day, Lawyer Terence McManus for the steamboat company conceded that no new life preservers were delivered to the *Slocum*. Elated at this concession, Mr. Garvan forged ahead with the questioning. He called the Reverend Mr. Schultz of Erie, Pennsylvania, Pastor Haas's guest, who told of the ordeal on the main afterdeck. He was followed by Benjamin Conklin, the chief engineer, who surprised the courtroom with a prompt "Here."

Conklin had been thought dead or missing. For some time, since John Wade of the tug *Wade* had sworn at the scene that "the engineer's a goner," and the *Evening Post* had stated that, "Chief Engineer George [*sic*] Conklin was burned at his post."

117

For his sudden disappearance and long absence Conklin offered no explanation but stated his name, position, and length of service on the *Slocum*. He had been with the ship since it was launched in 1891, and he had never heard of Section 2 of the Steamboat Inspection Service Rules and Regulations that steam pipes should lead from the boiler room "into the hold and different compartments thereof to extinguish fire." Mr. Garvan seized the moment to remind the court of Section 9: "No loose hay, loose cotton or loose hemp . . . coal oil, crude or refined petroleum . . . shall be carried as freight or used as stores." Then he went on with the questioning:

Q. — Who notified you of the fire?
A. — Mate Flanagan.
Q. — What did you do?
A. — I told my assistant to look after the engine, and I went to the donkey pump to work the water pressure.
Q. — Did you know the deck hose was not working?
A. — No, the pumps worked properly, and I thought the hose was all right.
Q. — What was the pressure on the pump?
A. — We had on about 28 pounds of steam, that would make about 50 or 60 pounds of water pressure on the hose.
Q. — Did you ever see any fire drills on the boat?
A. — No.

Conklin then said he did not leave his post at the pump until a rush of passengers carried him onto a tug that had come alongside — and, yes, he had gone about the vessel with Inspector Lundberg on May 5, and, no, no test had been made of the fire hose and standpipes.

William Trembley, a young deckhand, told of beating out the flames on a burning woman, donning a life belt, and jumping overboard with two children. He took refuge under the

118

paddle wheel, he said. He described the primitive struggle there: "My life preserver was pulled from me, and several who were struggling near me grabbed my arms and sank their teeth into them. I noticed a child was dangling about my head. It was being lowered into the water by a string — it looked like the strips of a shirt torn and tied together. . . . I noticed some kind of a float near me, and I got my two children safely on that. Then I swam back for the child dangling on the string, pulled it off, and also got it safely on the float. . . . I myself struggled for a while longer in the water, trying to land on some floating thing; then I lost consciousness. When I awoke, I was in the cabin of a tugboat."

After Trembley, Captain John Pease took the stand, wearing a frock coat and a long white beard. As captain of the Knickerbocker Company's flagship, the *Grand Republic,* it had been his duty to see to the needs of both vessels, and he seemed to view the *Slocum* as a tight ship ready for any season. He testified that he had overhauled the *General Slocum* in the spring, and swore that the lifeboats were "swung under davits" and that the life preservers "looked all right." He said that he had nothing to do with the life belts on the *Slocum,* though it was his duty to purchase them. This brought up the life-preserver controversy again.

Miss Hall, the company bookkeeper, had testified earlier that she had heard Captain Pease mention something about the *Slocum*'s needing life preservers, which led her to believe that the 250 billed to the *Grand Republic* were meant for the *Slocum.* Such was not the case, however; the *Slocum* did need new life belts, but Captain Pease needed them more — for his own ship.

Next Walter Payne, the porter, described the awful mess in the forward cabin and swore he put out the match he used to light his lantern there. "That boat went up in five minutes," he sputtered. *"Poof!* Just like a powder keg."

Tommy Ryan, the waiter, told of pulling down life belts,

119

throwing some to the crowd, then strapping one on Steward McGrann, the man who had just emptied the purser's safe. McGrann jumped overboard, he added.

"And was drowned, was he not?" the D.A. cut in.

"Yes," explained Ryan with compassion, "but he carried a heavy bag of money in his hand when he jumped."

Besides McGrann, it transpired, four other crewmen perished: Fireman John Tyson, Waiter Charles Wicker, Coffee Man Robert Lucas, and Pantryman Edward Smith.

A sensation of silent resentment swept through the hearing room when Mrs. Marie Behrens testified. The crowd, by now inured to — in fact, expecting — the worst, were momentarily disappointed when she stated that her daughter Annie was *saved* by the life belt she put on her — an instance unheard of till now. Then John Kircher took the stand, and it was the same old story again.

"The only one lost was the one who wore a life preserver," Kircher cried — the "only one" being his seven-year-old Elsie, on whom his wife had strapped a life belt. "Elsie . . . could not swim, although the other two [children] could, a little. Thinking the little girl would be safe with the preserver on the mother lifted her to the rail and dropped her over the side. She waited for Elsie to come up, but the child never appeared. She had sunk as though a stone were tied to her."

The day's hearing concluded with a display of bureaucratic obstinacy by Barrett and Fleming of the United States Steamboat Inspection Service.

Thomas H. Barrett, inspector of boilers for the Port of New York, was the first to confound the courtroom. Anticipating a question about "pipes . . . to carry steam into the hold . . . to extinguish fire," as provided for in Chapter 2 Section 2 of his department's Rules and Regulations, Mr. Barrett read a statement claiming the *General Slocum* had no "hold." Since it had no pipes — Mr. Barrett evidently assumed — it had no hold. A long wrangle ensued over the meaning of "hold." The hearing was suspended while dictionaries were found and consulted. The Century, Webster's, and most of the others agreed that the hold was the interior of a ship belowdecks, which was what District Attorney Garvan contended, but the phrase "especially the cargo deck of a ship" altered the argument in Mr. Barrett's favor. The *General Slocum* carried no cargo; therefore it had no cargo deck; therefore it had no hold. Mr. Barrett's inverse reasoning triumphed.

Following his chief, Assistant Inspector of Boilers John W. Fleming further frustrated the district attorney's efforts to prove that the *Slocum* had a hold by announcing that he was "very deaf," and proving it. Deafness, which can be a blessing in a boiler room, can be maddening in a courtroom, as Mr. Garvan was to discover. Fleming, after stating that he had tested the engines and boilers and found everything in first-class condition, leaned forward to hear the expected questions better. Raising his voice to a penetrating pitch and level, Garvan asked: "Didn't you find any forward compartment in your inspection?"

"I didn't go there at all!" Fleming shouted. "I don't know what is forward of the engine room or aft! I didn't go there!"

"Did the *Slocum* have any arrangement of valves leading from the boiler to any part of the ship to flood it in case of fire?" Garvan yelled. "No, sir," hollered Fleming, "because if she did it would be a mistake. She didn't need them!" District Attorney Garvan, almost in tears, gave up.

On the fourth day, Captain Van Schaick was again to testify. Unable to walk because of a fractured heel bone, he was carried through the hearing room on a stretcher to one of the back rooms, where, after a meeting of the D.A., the cornoner, and a doctor, it was decided that he be excused because of the pain he was still suffering. First Pilot Van Wart was called instead.

Van Wart, who had fared little better then the captain after their leap from the top deck, squirmed in pain as his injured spine adjusted to the sitting position. He said that he rang a jingle for full speed as he made for the island, a bell to slow up and another to stop, and that "the boat grounded easily without a jar." He also stated that "Captain Van Schaick gave the order to give the fire alarm when the flames appeared."

Whether an alarm was given could not be proved by Martin Kraljich, the youngest of the deckhands. When asked, "Did you hear a fire alarm rung?" the nineteen-year-old answered, "I wouldn't know one if I heard it."

Next, John L. Wade, engineer and owner of the tug *Wade*, hammered out his experiences on that awful day. Mrs. H. W. Turner described the life belts bursting at her touch and blinding her with powdered cork, and Paul Liebenow told of cutting his hands on the wire that held them up.

It was all too much — the stupidity, the cowardice, the greed, the horror, the terrible toll of lives. The jury had heard enough; it was ready to place the blame.

It was only Thursday. In the four days the jury sat, they had heard barely a quarter of the two hundred witnesses subpoenaed. How, Coroner Berry wondered, could they have heard enough? In disgust, he too was about to give it all up when an encouraging bit of news arrived: the *Slocum* had been raised.

On Friday, after a long conference with District Attorney Jerome, Assistant District Attorney Garvan, and United States District Attorney Burnett, Berry announced his determination to continue the inquest. Since the inquest was adjourned till Monday and the jury would *hear* no more evidence, he vowed they would at least *see* more. He had made arrangements for a tour of the East River, including a visit to the burned-out hulk.

The wreck of the *General Slocum* had lain at the bottom of the

East River for days before a move had been made to raise her. The Knickerbocker Steamboat Company had taken the $70,000 for which she was insured and resigned her to the insurance company, whose officers proceeded to haggle over the price of raising the hulk. The Merritt-Chapman Company wanted $10,000, the insurance company would pay only $5,000. Finally, after Mayor George McClellan and Police Commissioner McAdoo had visited the scene of the wreck, it was decided that the City of New York would take charge, with the Police Department having control during the operations necessary to raise the hull. In only four and a half days the Merritt-Chapman's four huge floating derricks had raised the wreck and beached it on the mud flats of Flushing Bay, from where it was taken, in a funeral flotilla, to the Erie Basin docks in Brooklyn.

The sight aboard the hulk was appalling. From the fantail looking forward, the jury saw, between the charred paddle box walls, a vast open space where the upper decks once had been. Not a beam or crosspiece remained; not a bulkhead or stanchion stood. A length of wire mesh that once held life belts above the main deck dangled from the starboard paddle-box wall. Forty feet above, two ladders hung from the gallows frame, groping for the top deck, no longer there.

At a signal from Coroner Berry, the jurymen moved forward over a carpet of water-soaked ashes, past the gallows frame and the boiler flues still standing, to the door of the forward cabin. As they gathered around a badly charred barrel brought up from below, Coroner Berry asked former Fire Marshal Thomas Freel, who was serving as an expert on the case, where the fire originated. Indicating the barrel at his side, Freel replied, "Inside this barrel."

Curiously, the barrel was still intact, though burned inside like the bowl of an old man's pipe. More curious was the condition of the forward cabin. A barrel of oil had not exploded,

123

some old life belts were not even scorched, some salt hay remained untouched. Evidently a carelessly flipped cigarette or match had ignited the hay in the barrel. It had burned straight upward until Coakley opened the door. Then the breeze from the open portholes was drawn across the barrel top, burning out the staves. While Coakley floundered about the cabin, its center became a furnace, its stairway a flue.

Satisfied that they had now seen enough, the jury boarded the police boat *Patrol* and with First Pilot Van Wart at the wheel went up the East River to follow the exact course taken by the *Slocum* twelve days before.

The next day, June 28, 1904, the inquest ended. After only three hours of deliberation the jury found the following men guilty of manslaughter in the second degree: President Frank Barnaby, Secretary James Atkinson, the directors of the Knickerbocker Steamboat Company, Captain John Pease, Assistant Inspector of Hulls Henry Lundberg, Captain William Van Schaick, and First Mate Ed Flanagan.

The inquest was over, the evidence in, the witnesses had been heard, the verdict given, but there was still time for some last-minute legal maneuvering. Two lawyers seized it for their clients' closing pleas.

Defense Attorney Dittenhoefer made the first move by requesting that his client be heard. At a nod from Coroner Berry a broken old man in a wheelchair was rolled down the aisle and lifted to the stand. After fitting his bruised body to the witness chair and pressing against the back for support, Captain William Van Schaick, for the first time, spoke at the inquest. Slowly, deliberately, sometimes almost in a murmur, he told the story as it happened in the pilothouse.

"I was in the pilothouse when the word was sent up that the boat was afire below. I told Van Wart to hold her to her course and ring for full speed ahead. I went out to see what the extent

124

of the trouble was, but I hardly got outside when I saw flames bursting up on the port side."

He came back inside, he said, and told Van Wart to head for North Brother Island. Where was the boat? "Just above Sunken Meadow between the red and black buoys." How far from the island? "A scant mile." How long till he reached the island? "Not over two and a half minutes. I want the jury to understand that a flood tide was running, and we were making . . . jacked up . . . fifteen or sixteen miles per hour. The fire came on like a locomotive . . . like a volcano." He left the ship only after it was beached, he said, "The pilot told me to jump . . . my hat caught fire. . . . I jumped thirty feet from the hurricane deck to the rocks below."

Exhausted, the captain paused for a moment to lift the pressure from his fractured heel. At this indication of pain, Attorney Dittenhoefer decided to play on the sympathy of the crowd. "How many passengers have you carried in your career as a captain?" he asked gently.

Taking the cue, Van Schaick replied, "I reckoned it up, and it is about thirty million people."

"And you carried them safely?"

The captain strained the credulity of everyone by replying, "I never had an accident."

Now, ex-Justice Julius Mayer, who was in court in the interest of Henry Lundberg, called his client to the stand. Lundberg, who had taken the Fifth Amendment throughout the hearing, had now been advised to tell all. What he told was a story of unbelievable dedication and unswerving devotion to duty.

On May 5, Lundberg said, he spent five and a half hours inspecting the *Slocum*; he examined the hull, the lifeboats, rafts, bulkheads, fire buckets, axes, hose and standpipes, *and* 2,550 life preservers. He said he found twenty-five bad ones and ordered them taken down. First he counted them, that took him one half hour; then he looked them over for four hours.

He felt them, tried the straps — he said. He admitted passing the fire hose without putting water through it and doing the same with the standpipe valves, but insisted the lifeboats were "swung under davits." He did not take any graft — he said.

Two weeks before, Lundberg had stated that on May 5 he counted the life belts and that there were at least 3,007 of them, all in good condition. "I did not reject one," he had said. Now, to conform somewhat to the testimony heard, Lundberg dropped the five hundred extra life belts he had said were aboard and upped the rejections to twenty-five. These were the only concessions he would make. Despite the overwhelming mass of evidence to the contrary, Lundberg would insist to the end that he inspected every life belt and found all but twenty-five "in good condition."

Pending hearings before a federal grand jury, Lundberg and First Mate Flanagan were held in $1,000 bail, the directors of the Knickerbocker Steamboat Company, President Barnaby, Secretary Atkinson, and Captain Pease were held in $5,000 bail each, as well as Captain Van Schaick.

At well after 9 P.M. the *General Slocum* inquest was adjourned.

THE FATE
OF THE CAPTAIN
AND HIS SHIP

ON JANUARY 10, 1906, Captain Van Schaick was placed on trial in the criminal branch of the United States Circuit Court in the Federal Building in New York City. He was charged with negligence, which, according to Section 5344 of the Revised Statutes, constitutes manslaughter when lives are lost.

The trial, like the inquest, was short-lived, occupying only three weeks on the court calendar. More witnesses were heard than at the inquest — over a dozen about the life belts alone — but for the most part there were the same people, the same stories; only the captain altered his testimony slightly by modifying his statement that he had never had an accident. He said that he had carried 25 or 30 million passengers in over thirty years "without a loss of life."

On January 27, despite the contention of his lawyer that the government had failed to prove intentional and willful neglect

127

on the part of the captain, the jury found him guilty of negligence. Of the three counts against him, the jury could not agree on the first two: the death of Michael McGrann, the steward, and the death of a "Rachel Roe." On the third, however, they were unanimous: guilty of not holding fire drills, not training the crew properly, and not maintaining the proper fire apparatus aboard. There was no recommendation for mercy, and the presiding judge gave none. Judge Thomas merely intoned a judicial cliché: "You are no ordinary criminal; I must make an example of you." He sentenced the captain to ten years in jail.

The words and sentence seem harsh when applied to a contrite old man, but the captain had neglected his duty, and over a thousand people *were* dead.

Captain Van Schaick was the only one of the indicted men to be convicted. Indeed, only Henry Lundberg, the steamboat inspector, was even brought to trial. U.S. District Attorney Henry Burnett, determined as he was, could not get a conviction in Lundberg's case. He tried three times and failed.

It is hard to see how one jury could find Van Schaick guilty of negligence, yet three could not find Lundberg negligent, too. Certainly, if the captain had not maintained the equipment properly, the inspector had not inspected it properly. It was as simple as that. But juries are not always logical.

As for the others indicted with the captain — Flanagan, Barnaby, Atkinson, Pease, and the directors of the Knickerbocker Steamboat Company — they were all but forgotten.

On April 6, 1906, the Harbor Master and Pilots Association collected $1,000 for a retrial because they, like thousands of others, thought Van Schaick had been made the scapegoat. But no retrial was granted. Instead the captain was set free on $10,000 bail pending the appeal of his case.

On February 12, 1908, the appeal was denied by the United States Court of Appeals, and the captain was required to serve his ten years — in Sing Sing.

Fortunately the captain, while out on bail, had wooed and married (he was then seventy years old) the woman who had nursed him back to health. Forty-year-old Grace Mary Spratt, superintendent of nurses at the Lebanon Hospital where the captain had convalesced, was now the superintendent of his affairs — and lucky for him. As his wife, she campaigned tirelessly for his release and pardon. After two petitions had been refused by President Theodore Roosevelt, a third with 250,000 names brought a favorable response from President William Howard Taft. In August 1911, after serving three and a half years of his sentence, Captain Van Schaick was paroled and on Christmas Day pardoned.

When the Captain left Sing Sing, he was given $5,620 from a fund raised by pilots, captains, and his many other friends, with which he bought a farm at Perth, Fulton County, New York, where his wife helped him toward a new life. He died one day after his ninetieth birthday, on December 8, 1927.

If fate had been harsh to the captain, it was no less harsh to his ship. On December 4, 1911, three months after the captain was paroled, the once proud *General Slocum* met her end.

Now a lowly barge called the *Maryland* she was being towed by the tug *Asher J. Hudson* from Camden to Newark, New Jersey, with a load of coke. Off Ludlam Beach, in heavy weather, she sprung a leak. The tug captain, Robert Moon, realizing the gale was too much for him with a barge in tow, took off his crew and cut her loose.

Abandoned once again, the *General Slocum* foundered in twenty-four feet of water off Corson's Inlet, about seventeen miles south of Atlantic City. On hearing of the loss, the owner, Peter Hagen, sighed with relief. Bad luck had continued to hound the vessel. She was always springing leaks and needing repairs, and just before the last trip he had had to install a new rudder. "Ill fortune always followed her," he said, "She was always getting into trouble. . . . I'm glad she's gone."

THE REPORT

ON JUNE 23, 1904, before the coroner's inquest had completed its hearings, President Theodore Roosevelt appointed a five-man commission to investigate the causes of the *General Slocum* disaster and to make recommendations as to future action.

The commission consisted of Lawrence O. Murray, assistant Secretary of Commerce and Labor, Herbert Knox Smith, deputy commissioner of corporations, and George Uhler, supervising inspector general of the Steamboat Inspection Service, Brig. Gen. John M. Wilson, U.S. Army retired, and Navy Commander Cameron Winslow. Mr. Murray was appointed chairman and was to report to the then Secretary of Commerce and Labor, George B. Cortelyou.

After holding hearings in New York City and Washington, D.C., between July 19 and September 27, the commission met in one final session in Washington on October 4, 1904, and issued its "Report of the United States Commission of Investigation Upon the Disaster to the Steamer 'General Slocum'." The report placed the responsibility for the disaster largely upon the officers of the Steamboat Inspection Service.

The reasons for the apparent inefficiency of the service, said the report, were an inadequate corps of inspectors at the Port of New York, inadequate supervision by the supervising inspectors and local inspectors over the assistant inspectors, and the reluctance of owners of vessels to maintain lifesaving and fire-fighting equipment in proper condition.

On October 12 the President indicated his approval of the report and ordered that all officers of the service who had been concerned in the *Slocum* affair dismissed for "laxity and neglect in performing their duties." Five men were fired — assistant inspectors Lundberg and Fleming, plus the supervising inspector of the Second District (northeast region) of the United States, Dumont L. Barrett, and two local inspectors of the port of New York.

The supervising inspector general was spared, and Secretary Cortelyou was found to be above reproach. Indeed, just three weeks before the disaster, he had had Department Circular No. 44 distributed throughout the USSIS, which warned inspectors to be especially careful in checking all equipment and particularly to "take special precautions to prevent the overcrowding of steamers."

On July 7, the Secretary ordered reinspection of 268 ferryboats, steamers, and excursion vessels under its jurisdiction. The reinspection report was dismaying. Among all classes of vessel, 18 percent of the life preservers supposed to be on board could not be counted on, because they were either defective or short of the number required, and 18 percent of the fire hose was defective as well. Broken down into five classes, the report was even more startling. Oceangoing steamers were rated in the best condition as regards life preservers and second as to fire hose. Inland steamers were second as regards life preservers and fourth as to hose. Towing steamers (tugboats) were third as to both life preservers and hose. Ferryboats were fourth as regards life preservers and first as to hose, whereas excursion boats were in the worst shape — fifth as regards both life preservers and hose, showing a deficiency of 33 percent in life preservers and over 26 percent in fire hose. But that was not all. The most shocking part of the commission's report came next: the construction of passenger steamers.

The Commission feels that it cannot emphasize this matter too strongly. So far as the passengers were concerned, the entire disaster to the *General Slocum* took place in less than twenty minutes. When the flames were once well under way, nothing could stop them, as the vessel was simply a shell of highly combustible, frequently painted, extremely dry wood — a mere tinder box of the greatest possible inflammability.

The sole protection of such a vessel against fire depends on prompt extinguishment at its early inception. If such extinguishment be rendered impossible by any one of a large number of possible causes, to wit, failure of the hose, lack of discipline of crew, failure of pumps, or any one of a number of possible minor defects in machinery, there is no reason why the disaster to the *General Slocum* might not be duplicated on any one of hundreds of similar vessels still running in New York Harbor and elsewhere. The steamer *General Slocum* was *not abnormal*; it was *typical*, and these facts must be plainly recognized if the lives of passengers on such boats are to be at all properly safeguarded.

The sixty-two-page report then went on to recommend certain changes in statute law, departmental and bureau regulations, and in the conditions in the Steamboat Inspection Service. It urged that, in the construction of passenger vessels, the building material be changed from wood to metal wher-

132

ever possible, especially in the construction of fireproof bulkheads (walls) to contain fires in the area where they start. As to life belts, one was to be carried aboard steamers for every passenger and member of the crew (a point not stressed in earlier regulations), and they were to be of sturdy material and tested aboard the vessels and their age noted at each inspection. Fire hose was to be of material that would not lose its strength from the time of one inspection to another and strong enough to withstand a pressure of 100 pounds per square inch, and all hose couplings on the same ship were to be of the same size and of the same thread so as to be interchangeable. Steam pipes were to be inserted into cargo or freight holds to carry steam from the boilers into those compartments to extinguish fire, and finally it was recommended that lifeboats should be secured in such a way as to be easily and quickly cast adrift.

It was ironic that all these fervent recommendations were merely restatements of the rules and regulations already on the books of the Steamboat Inspection Service since 1871. The *Slocum* disaster could not have happened if these regulations had merely been enforced.

It was plain that the fault was not with the equipment but with the men, the maintainers. Who then was responsible? The commission found this part of the report the most difficult to write.

It noted that, under the then law, the responsibility for defective equipment tended to fall wholly on the captain — an unfair imposition. Theoretically, the captain should not take the vessel from the dock if he knows that there is defective equipment aboard, but in practice the captain who refused to sail for this reason would be promptly fired by the owner. Consequently captains take the burden of this responsibility upon themselves. Instead, the report maintained, the owners or corporate owners should be held answerable for vessels that navigate with defective equipment.

The existing law also gave no definition of the duties of the captain or other licensed officers and did not require mates to be licensed at all, except on oceangoing vessels. The report recommended that a licensed deck officer be mandatory on board all passenger steamers *and especially on excursion steamers*. It was clear from evidence before the commission that the crews of excursion boats were of a very low grade and therefore should be given frequent fire drills and other such disciplines to overcome their original lack of skills. Impressed with the special helplessness of passengers carried on excursion steamers because of the presence of a large percentage of women and children, the commission also suggested that extra uniformed deckhands or watchmen, trained in crowd management, should be required on such vessels.

Finally, the report went on to say that the duties of steamboat inspectors were not clearly defined either, and, what was more, that they were powerless. They had no authority to order worthless safety appliances destroyed after condemnation or to prevent their being used again. They had no power to revoke licenses upon discovery of violations aboard a vessel, no power to require fire and boat drills, and, worst of all, no power to order the inspection of a vessel. The inspections were left up to the owners, who could apply for them voluntarily if they pleased. This, of course, made the maintenance of the entire USSIS little better than a farce.

Inspectors should be given police power over steamboats, to enforce the requirements of law and regulations, plus a sufficient force of men to manage the work. Certificates of inspection were to be signed by the men who did the actual examination of the boat and not by their supervisors — and only after they had tested every piece of safety equipment under operating conditions. Finally the commission recommended that inspectors' salaries be fixed at standard yearly amounts and not be dependent on the number of inspections they carried out.

All the changes recommended by the Commission of Investigation were eventually brought about by the reorganization of the inspection service and by subsequent legislation. The inspection service was later renamed the Bureau of Marine Inspection and Navigation, and in 1942 it was placed under the jurisdiction of the Treasury Department and its seagoing division, the United States Coast Guard.

APPENDIX

GENERAL SLOCUM STATISTICS

Gross tonnage	1,281
Net tonnage	1,013
Draft	7½ to 8½ feet
Length, overall	264 feet
Length, hull	255 feet
Keel	230 feet
Hull, depth	12 feet 3 inches
Hull, beam	37 feet
Beam, outside guards	64 feet
Hogback frames, length	142 feet
Paddle wheels	31 feet in diameter
Paddles (26)	9 feet wide
Boilers (2)	12½ feet by 9 feet 5 inches by 23 feet 7 inches
Piston cylinder	20 feet high by 53 inches in diameter
Piston stroke	12 feet
Main deck saloon	100 by 50 feet
Women's cabin, main deck	65 by 50 feet
Promenade deck saloon	100 by 50 feet

Safety Equipment

6 Lifeboats, all metal, 22 feet 3 inches by 6 feet 1 inch by 2 feet 3 inches
2 Barstow life rafts
2 Cylinder life rafts
2 Fire pumps, hand-operated, 4 by 8 capacity, double acting
1 Fire pump, steam-operated, 8-inch diameter of plunger, 12-inch stroke of 603 cubic inch capacity
400 feet 2½-inch hose
200 feet 1½-inch hose
2 Standpipes, forward main deck
90 Water buckets
3 Water barrels
4 Water tanks
10 Fire axes
2,250 Life preservers

ROSTER OF THE CREW

NAME	AGE	POSITION
Van Schaick, Wm. H.	60 (67)	Captain
Van Wart, Edward	62	1st Pilot
Weaver, Edwin. N.	28	2nd Pilot
Conklin, B. Frank	39	Chief Engineer
Brandow, Everett	34	2nd Engineer
Flanagan, Edward	27	1st Mate
Corcoran, James	20	2nd Mate
Brennan, John N.	48	Deckhand
Coakley, John J.	30	Deckhand
Collins, Thomas	25	Deckhand
Kraljich, Martin	19	Deckhand
O'Neill, Daniel	24	Deckhand
Trembley, Wm.	33	Deckhand
Lee, Michael	46	Fireman
Mullen, Patrick	24	Fireman
Silveria, Frank	32	Fireman
*Tyson, John	39 (died)	Fireman
Gaffga, Elbert J.	20	Oiler
Canfield, Henry	53	Negro cook
Robinson, Edwin	19	Negro 2nd cook
Wood, James	45	Dishwasher
Freeman, Jenny E.	33	Stewardess (Negro)
Hubschman, Morris	39	Waiter
Leonard, Paul C.	24	Waiter
*Lucas, Robert	32 (died)	Coffee man (Negro)
Owens, George	39	Chowder man
Payne, Walter	22	Porter (Negro)
Plintin, James	22	Captain's waiter (Negro)
Potar, Lewis	39	Bartender
*McGrann, Michael	48 (died)	Steward
Ryan, Thomas	28	Waiter
*Smith, Edward	68 (died)	Pantryman (Negro)
Smith, Bessie	35	Stewardess (Negro)
Volze, George	39	2nd Bartender
*Wicker, Charles	54 (died)	Waiter
Wubber, William	34	Waiter

BIBLIOGRAPHY

Bascom, Willard, *Waves and Beaches*. New York: Doubleday & Co., 1964.

Bliven, Bruce, *Battle for Manhattan*. New York: Henry Holt, 1956.

Boyle, Robert H., *The Hudson River*. New York: W.W. Norton & Co., 1969.

Bradley, David L., *Bradley's Reminiscences of New York Harbor and Complete Water Front Directory of New York, Brooklyn and New Jersey*. New York: 1896.

Brown, Alexander C., "Paddlebox Decorations of American Sound Steamboats." *The American Neptune*, Vol. III, No. 1 (1943).

Bullock, Seymour, "History of Steam Navigation." *Connecticut Magazine*, Vol. 9 (1905).

Casson, Herbert N., "The Story of the *General Slocum* Disaster." *Munsey's Magazine*, Vol. 32 (1904).

Churchill, Alan, *Park Row*. New York: Rhinehart & Co., Inc., 1958.

Fletcher, A., "River, Lake, Bay and Sound Steamers of the United States." *Naval Architectural and Marine Engineering Magazine*, Vol. 10 (May 1916).

Hanson, John Wesley, Jr., *New York's Awful Excursion Boat Horror*. Chicago: 1904.

Lane, Carl. *American Paddle Steamboats*. New York: Coward-McCann, 1943.

McAdam, Roger W., *Commonwealth, Giantess of the Sound*. New York: Stephan Daye Press, 1959.

———, *The Old Fall River Line*. Baltimore, Md.: Stephen Daye Press, 1937.

———, *Priscilla of Fall River*. New York: Stephan Daye Press, 1947.

Morrison, J. H., *History of New York Shipyards*. New York: W. F. Sametz & Co., 1909.

———, *History of American Steam Navigation*. New York: W. F. Sametz & Co., 1903.

New York City Board of Health, *Annual Report of 1904*. New York: Martin Press, 1905.

New York City Department of Health, "Description of Clothing and Bodies." Dr. Higgins, Coroner's Office, New York (June 22, 1904).

New York City Department of Public Charities. *Annual Report of 1904*. New York: Martin Brown Press, 1905.

New York Yacht Club, *N.Y. Yacht Club Yearbook*. New York: 1905.

Northrup, H.D., *New York's Awful Steamboat Horror*. Philadelphia, Pa.: National Co., 1904.

Ogilvie, John S., *History of the* General Slocum *Disaster*. New York: Ogilvie Co., 1904.

Payne, Alice, *City Island, Tales of the Clam Diggers*. New York: 1969.

Phelps-Stokes, I. N., *The Iconography of Manhattan Island*. New York: R. H. Dodd. 1915–1928.

Richardson, James. "The Unbarring of Hellgate." New York: *Century Magazine* (Nov. 1, 1871).

St. Mark's Evan. Lutheran Church. *Journal for the Seventeenth Annual Excursion of St. Mark's Evangelical Lutheran Church*. New York: 1904.

Serrell, James E., *Memorial of James E. Serrell in Relation to a New East River and the Filling of Hellgate*. New York: 1867.

———, *Plan and Description Proposing to Re-Model the City of New York and its Vicinity*. New York: 1869.

Sierichs, Anna, Letters to the Author by Anna Sierichs (née Frese) (August–November 1968).

Stebbins, Nathaniel L., *The Illustrated Coast Pilot*. Boston: N. L. Stebbins, 1896.

U. S. Civil Service Commission. *Information Concerning Examination for Entrance to the Steamboat Inspection Service*. Washington, D.C.: Government Printing Office, 1904.

U.S. Coast Guard. *Laws Governing Marine Inspection*. Washington, D.C.: Government Printing Office, 1950.

U.S. Congress. House Committee on Claims, "Bill H.R. 4154 for the Relief of the Victims of the *General Slocum* Disaster." Washington, D.C.: Government Printing Office, 1910.

U.S. General Slocum Disaster Investigation Commission, *Report of the United States Commission of the Investigation Upon the Disaster to the Steamer* General Slocum. *October 8, 1904*. Washington, D.C.: Government Printing Office, 1904.

U.S. Steamboat Inspection Service, *Annual Report of the Supervising Inspector General*. Washington, D.C.: U.S. Government Printing Office, 1877 to 1910.

———, *Catalogue of Books and Blanks Used by the U.S. Steamboat Inspection Service*. Washington, D.C.: Government Printing Office, 1912.

———, *General Rules and Regulations*. Washington, D.C.: U.S. Government Printing Office, 1871.

———, *General Rules and Regulations*. Washington, D.C.: Government Printing Office, 1904.

U.S. War Department, *Survey of the East River and Hellgate*. Washington, D. C.: U.S. Government Printing Office, 1913.

Van Pelt, Daniel. *Leslie's History of Greater New York*. New York: Arkell Publishing Co., 1898.

The World. *The World Almanac and Encyclopedia*. New York: The Press Publishing Co., New York World, 1905.

INDEX

Abendschein, Mary, chairwoman of picnic committee, 18
Atkinson, James, company secretary: verdict of guilt, manslaughter, 124; bail, 126; no trial, 128

Backman, Mrs., dead passenger, 70 *(illus.)*
Balzer, Nicholas, passenger, 50 – 51, 101
Barnaby, Frank, company president: inquest testimony, 110 – 12; verdict of guilt, manslaughter, 124; bail, 126; no trial, 128
Barrett, Thomas, inspector: inquest testimony, 120 – 21
Behrens, Mrs. Marie, passenger: inquest testimony, 120
Berry, Joseph, Bronx coroner, 109, 122 – 23
Brandow, Everett, 2nd engineer, 22, 23, 140; in fire, 41, 84; inquest testimony, 113 – 14

Canfield, Henry, cook, 23; in fire, 86
Coakley, John, deckhand, 22, 28, 33, 35, 140; in fire, 36, 40 – 41, 46, 85, 124; criticisms of actions, 43 *(note)*; at inquest, 106 *(illus.)*, testimony, 112 – 13
Collins, Thomas, deckhand, 140; in fire, 41
Conklin, Ben, chief engineer, 22 – 23, 27, 140; inspection, 9 – 10; in fire, 41 – 42, 83, 84 – 85; inquest testimony, 117 – 18
Corcoran, James, 2nd mate, 140; in fire, 40, 42, 46; inquest testimony, 113
Coroner's inquest, *see* Inquest, coroner's

Dougherty, James (Department of Public Charities), 102 – 3

145

Dumont, James, inspector: inquest testimony, 116

Ell, John, passenger, 56 – 57
Everett, Charles P., diver: report of rescue operations, 96 – 98
Excursions and vessels, *1904*, 2 – 3

Federal Investigation Commission hearings on inspection, 131 – 36; report and recommendations, 132 – 36
Fire hoses, in Federal Investigation Commission hearings, 133; in inquest, 111, 114 – 15, 118, 125; inspection of, 10
Flanagan, Edward, first mate, 21 – 22, 140; inspections, 9 – 10; in fire, 40 – 41, 42, 59, 87, 99, 118; panic of, 83 – 84; in rescue operations, 73 – 74, 82; inquest testimony, 113; verdict of manslaughter, 124; bail, 126; no trial, 128
Fleming, John W., inspector, 9; inquest testimony, 121; dismissal, 132
Frese, Anna, passenger, 45 – 46, 53 – 54

Gailing, Louise, passenger, 54 – 55
Garvan, Francis P., assistant district attorney: at inquest, 110 – 111, 114 – 115, 118, 121 – 122
General Slocum: anchored on the Hudson, 12 *(illus.)*; building of (1891), 3 – 4; close-up, 12 *(illus.)*; crew roster, 140 *(table)*; early excursions and accidents to, *1891 – 1902,* 4 – 8; federal inspection (1904) by U.S. Steamboat Inspection Service, 3, 8 – 10; in inquest, 110 – 11, 116 – 17, 120 – 21; rounding the Battery, 13 *(illus.)*; safety equipment, 139 *(table)*; seen against Manhattan skyline, early 1900's, 11 *(illus.)*; statistics, 139 *(table)*
General Slocum, aftermath of fire: as *Maryland,* foundering of, 129 – 130; beaching and sinking of wreck, 95 – 96; Federal Investigation Commission hearings, 131 – 36; inquest, coroner's, 109 – 26, *see also* Inquest, coroner's; raising of, 123 – 24, raised hulk, Frontispiece illus., 66 *(illus.)*, 95; trial of captain, 127 – 30, *see also under* Van Schaick, William
General Slocum, excursion: boarding of passengers, 23, 25 – 28; passing of Hell's Gate and discovery of fire, 30 – 31; preparations of crew, 20 – 23; preparations on morning of, 18 – 19; route, 23, 26 – 27, 38 – 39 *(map)*; route before fire, 30 – 34
General Slocum, fire: acts of crew members, 83 – 86; alarm sounded, 37, 39; chronology of developments, 35 – 93; collapse of decks, 64 – 65, 66 *(illus.)*, 93; discovery and explosion, 33 – 34, 36; eyewitness drawing, 63 *(illus.)*; fire hoses, failure of, 41 – 42; hay in cabin afire, 36; life preservers, failure of, 47, 51, 83 – 89; passengers' accounts, 45 – 46, 49 – 62; spread of, chronology, 9:57 – 10:07, 35 – 43; stampede of passengers, 42 – 43, 64 – 65 *(illus.)*; time, 22 minutes, 83, 94, 133
dead, the: coffins, 102 – 104; collection of, 98 – 100; crew deaths, 95, 103, 120, 140, funeral procession, 72 *(illus.)*; funerals and burials, 104; memorial, 108 *(illus.)*; morgue, bodies in, identification, 102 – 3; recovery of bodies, 95 – 98; relations and friends at morgue, 70 *(illus.)*; response of neighbors and relatives, 101 – 2; temporary morgue at pier, 71 *(illus.)*; unidentified, burial of, 104
rescue operations, 73 – 82; by boats, 73 – 78, 81 – 82; by doctors and nurses, 68 – 69 *(illus.)*; by police, 78 – 79; Diver Everett's report, 96 – 98; failure of boats to assist, 79 – 81; policemen carrying

corpses, 67 *(illus.)*; Riverside Hospital staff, 90– 92; robberies, 92; survivors, 68– 69 *(illus.)*

Haas, Rev. George, pastor of St. Mark's, 14 *(illus.)*; on excursion, 27– 28, 30; in fire, 45, 57, 86, 101– 2, family, 60– 61

Hall, Josephine, company bookkeeper, 107 *(illus.)*; juggling of bills for life preservers, inquest testimony, 112, 114, 119

Hay in cabin, 19, 85; in inquest, 123– 24

Heinz, George, passenger, 49– 50

Hencken, Lucy, passenger, 54– 55

Hoffman family, 55– 56

Inquest, coroner's, 109– 26; bail, 126; crew, testimony of, 112– 22; exhibits, 110; jury, 105 *(illus.)*, selection, 109; verdict of seven guilty of second degree manslaughter, 124; visit to wreck, 122– 24; passengers injured, testimony, 110, 120; witnesses' testimony, 110

Inspection, federal, 3, 8– 10; in inquest, 110– 111, 116– 17, 120– 21; *see also Federal Investigation Commission; U.S. Steamboat Inspection Service*

Kassebaum, Mrs. Catherine, passenger, 57– 59, 86

Kircher, John, passenger: inquest testimony, 120

Knickerbocker Steamboat Company, owners of *General Slocum,* 3– 4; officers, testimony at inquest, 110– 12

Kraljich, Martin, deckhand, 140; inquest testimony, 122

Lee, Michael, fireman, 140; in fire, 86

Life boats: inspection, 10; in inquest, 110, 113– 14; number of, 139 *(table)*

Life preservers: in Federal Investigation Commission hearings, 133; in inquest, 107 *(illus.)*, 110– 11, 113– 14, 117– 19, 122– 23, 125– 26; in

Van Schaick trial, 127; inspection, 9– 10; number of, 139 *(table)*

Life rafts: number of, 139 *(table)*

Lucas, Robert, coffee man: death, 140

Lundberg, Henry, inspector: *1904* inspection, 9– 10; at inquest, 105 *(illus.)*, 107 *(illus.)*; testimony, 115– 17, 125– 26; verdict of guilt, manslaughter, 123; bail, 126; trial, 126

McGrann, Michael, steward, 140; death, 87, 119– 20, 128, 139

McManus, Terence, company attorney: at inquest, 112, 117

Maurer, George, bandleader, 29; family in fire, 59– 60

Maurer's Band, 27, 29– 30, 34; in fire, 59– 60

Muth family, passengers, 70 *(illus.)*

Oettinger, Willie, passenger, 100– 1

O'Gorman, coroner, 106 *(illus.)*

O'Neill, Daniel, deckhand, 19, 21, 140; in fire, 40, 85; inquest testimony, 113– 14

Owens, James J., observer of fire, 89– 90

Payne, Walter, porter, 20– 21, 140; in fire, 40, 42, 86; inquest testimony, 119

Pease, John, captain: inquest testimony, 119; verdict of guilt, manslaughter, 124; bail, 126; no trial, 128

Robinson, Edwin, cook, 23, 140; in fire, 86

Ryan, Tommy, waiter, 140; inquest testimony, 119– 20

St. Mark's Evangelical Lutheran Church, 13 *(illus.)*; parish and neighborhood (Little Germany), 15– 18; Pastor, *see* Haas, Rev. George
   excursion, seventeenth annual: charter of *General Slocum,* 15; boarding, Third Street Pier, 25– 28; number of passengers,

28; preparations of passengers before boarding, 23–26; program welcoming passengers, 14 *(illus.)*, 29–30

Schneider, August and family, passengers, 29; in fire, 59–60

Schultz, Rev. George: in fire, 61; inquest testimony, 117

Slocum, Major General Henry Warner; naming of boat for, 4

Smith, Edward, pantry man: death, 140

Trembley, William, deckhand, 140; inquest testimony, 118–19

Tyson, John, fireman: death, 140

U.S. Steamboat Inspection Service (USSIS): Federal Investigation Commission report and recommendations, 132–36; in inquest, 110–11, 116–17, 120–21; inspection of *General Slocum* (1904), 3, 8–10; reorganization, 136; testimony of inspectors at inquest, 115–17

Van Schaick, William, captain, 7, 140; on excursion, 30, 32; in fire, 42–43, 43 *(note)*, 47, 49, 83; account of fire, 99–100; arrest, 100; at inquest, 106 *(illus.)*, 121, verdict of guilt, 124, testimony, 124–25, bail, 126; trial, 127–30, conviction and sentence, 128, retrial not granted, 128, freed on bail, 128, sentence of ten years, 128–29, campaign for release, 129, parole, 129

Van Tassel, Albert, police officer, 88–89

Van Wart, Edward, 1st pilot, 26, 140; on excursion, 30, 32; in fire, 37–38, 42–43, 47–49, 82, 124; inquest testimony, 121–22

Wade, John L., engineer, 81–82, 140; inquest testimony, 117, 122

Weaver, Edwin N., 2nd pilot, 140; on excursion, 30, 32; in fire, 32, 35, 42; arrest, 100; inquest testimony, 114–15

Weber family: in fire, 36, 51–53

Wicker, Charles, waiter: death, 140

148